SEAL'S GOAL

SHARON HAMILTON

Copyright © 2018 by Sharon Hamilton
Print Edition

All rights reserved. Without limiting the rights under copyright reserved above, no part of this publication may be reproduced, stored in or introduced into a retrieval system, or transmitted, in any form, or by any means (electronic, mechanical, photocopying, recording, or otherwise) without the prior written permission of the copyright owner of this book.

This is a work of fiction. Names, characters, places, brands, media, and incidents are either the product of the author's imagination or are used fictitiously. In many cases, liberties and intentional inaccuracies have been taken with rank, description of duties, locations and aspects of the SEAL community.

SHARON HAMILTON'S BOOK LIST

SEAL BROTHERHOOD SERIES
Accidental SEAL (Book 1)
Fallen SEAL Legacy (Book 2)
SEAL Under Covers (Book 3)
SEAL The Deal (Book 4)
Cruisin' For A SEAL (Book 5)
SEAL My Destiny (Book 6)
SEAL Of My Heart (Book 7)
Fredo's Dream (Book 8)
SEAL My Love (Book 9)
SEAL Brotherhood Box Set 1 (Accidental SEAL & Prequel)
SEAL Brotherhood Box Set 2 (Fallen SEAL & Prequel)
Ultimate SEAL Collection Vol. 1 (Books 1-4 + 2 Prequels)
Ultimate SEAL Collection Vol. 2 (Books 5-7)

BAD BOYS OF SEAL TEAM 3 SERIES
SEAL's Promise (Book 1)
SEAL My Home (Book 2)
SEAL's Code (Book 3)
Big Bad Boys Bundle (Books 1-3 of Bad Boys)

BAND OF BACHELORS SERIES
Lucas (Book 1) *Available Only*
by Audio, Bundle, or Newsletter
Alex (Book 2)
Jake (Book 3)
Jake 2 (Book 4)
Big Band of Bachelors Bundle

TRUE BLUE SEALS SERIES
True Navy Blue (prequel to Zak)
Zak (Includes novella above)

NASHVILLE SEAL SERIES
Nashville SEAL (Book 1)
Nashville SEAL: Jameson (Books 1 & 2 combined)

SILVER SEALS
SEAL Love's Legacy

SLEEPER SEALS
Bachelor SEAL

NEW STAND ALONES
SEAL's Goal: The Beautiful Game
Love Me Tender, Love You Hard

BONE FROG BROTHERHOOD SERIES
New Year's SEAL Dream (Book 1)
SEALed At The Altar (Book 2)

PARADISE SERIES
Paradise: In Search of Love

STANDALONE NOVELLAS
SEAL You In My Dreams (Magnolias and Moonshine)
SEAL Of Time (Trident Legacy)

FALL FROM GRACE SERIES (PARANORMAL)
Gideon: Heavenly Fall

GOLDEN VAMPIRES OF TUSCANY SERIES (PARANORMAL)
Honeymoon Bite (Book 1)
Mortal Bite (Book 2)

THE GUARDIANS (PARANORMAL)
Heavenly Lover (Book 1)
Underworld Lover (Book 2)
Underworld Queen (Book 3)

AUDIOBOOKS
Sharon Hamilton's books are available as audiobooks narrated by J.D. Hart.

ABOUT THE BOOK

Professional Goalkeeper Patrick Harrington comes home to the U.S. from England to attend the funeral of his best friend, Navy SEAL Ryan Rosen. Ryan's fiancée is the girl who got away, the one he's been in love with ever since he set eyes on her in first grade.

Stephanie Carter's world turns on its axis when Ryan is removed from her life, but not from her heart. Ryan's best friend, Patrick, becomes her path to healing the Trident-shaped hole left behind.

Compassion leads to passion as they find the possibility of a life together neither one planned, or ever dreamed could exist. Will Patrick's decision to join the Teams destroy their love and will her heart be able to handle a second loss?

Patrick begins his first deployment to Central Africa, to extract or immobilize a powerful warlord who is terrorizing and spreading his brand of hate. With the outbreak of Ebola, the stakes are suddenly higher. But Patrick will soon learn how interconnected the whole world is. He comes face to face with pure evil, and retribution for the past. He learns the value of what he's fighting for.

AUTHOR'S NOTE

I always dedicate my SEAL Brotherhood books to the brave men and women who defend our shores and keep us safe. Without their sacrifice, and that of their families—because a warrior's fight always includes his or her family—I wouldn't have the freedom and opportunity to make a living writing these stories. They sometimes pay the ultimate price, so we can debate, argue, go have coffee with friends, raise our children and see them have children of their own.

One of my favorite tributes to warriors resides on many memorials, including one I saw honoring the fallen of WWII on an island in the Pacific:

> "When you go home
> Tell them of us, and say
> For your tomorrow,
> We gave our today."

These are my stories created out of my own imagination. Anything that is inaccurately portrayed is either my mistake, or done intentionally to disguise something I might have overheard over a beer or in the corner of one of the hangouts along the Coronado Strand.

I support two main charities. Navy SEAL/UDT Museum operates in Ft. Pierce, Florida. Please learn about this wonderful museum, all run by active and former SEALs and their friends and families, and who rely on public support, not that of the U.S. Government.
www.navysealmuseum.org

I also support Wounded Warriors, who tirelessly bring together the warrior as well as the family members who are just learning to deal with their soldier's condition and have nowhere to turn. It is a long path to becoming well, but I've seen first-hand what this organization does for its warriors and the families who love them. Please give what your heart tells you is right. If you cannot give, volunteer at one of the many service centers all over the United States. Get involved. Do something meaningful for someone who gave so much of themselves, to families who have paid the price for your freedom. You'll find a family there unlike any other on the planet.
www.woundedwarriorproject.org

CHAPTER 1

PATRICK HARRINGTON STARED out the bus window at the bevy of pretty ladies who always congregated at the player entrance, which looked like a cage. The Seattle facility wasn't as bad as those in Europe, where women frequently were in and out of the locker room. In the States, only female sports reporters were allowed in. But the steel barriers meant to keep out the public still felt like prison bars.

Several of the guys on his team were looking forward to a session with the local female newscaster, who liked to interview them naked. Her sultry voice gave them commando hard-ons. Patrick always figured she had a serious kinky streak, but she really wasn't his style.

The girls hanging around the bus today appeared a bit haggard. He liked his women athletic, but not too skinny. He liked wholesome girls who enjoyed sex and were quiet about it. Well, they didn't have to be quiet in bed, just not ones to go blabbing to the press.

The Tottenham squad strutted their stuff, ambling through the gauntlet of women, carrying their more important personal gear while the team handlers lugged all the heavy equipment. Patrick never left a stadium without his gloves, and his backup gloves, and the ones that could be back up to the backup ones. And he was never without the red, white, and blue American flag Duck Tape he used to hold up his shin guards and tape his ball-handlers in place. His Brit coach didn't like it, and because he'd been so vocal in the rebukes aimed at Patrick, the rest of the team, consisting of mostly African and Eastern European players, adopted the Duck Tape too, just for spite. Patrick was not the team captain, but he was the team moral leader, especially when it came to minding stupid rules.

Duck Tape was essential because Velcro could be ripped with a set of cleats…but Duck Tape? Duck Tape was the bomb. Not only was it good for the game, it was good for other antics, and since he bought it by the case and had it shipped from Ohio, he always had lots of it on hand.

Phone numbers were being exchanged between the players and fangirls behind him while the rest of Tottenham first team descended the ramp, way down into the bowels of the Seattle Sounders stadium. A few VIP fans had been allowed to wait for them outside the changing room, to applaud the team's arrival. The British Consulate-General and his wife had flown up from San Francisco to watch the game. They and several other dignitaries and friends of the Sounders' ownership, as well as major investors in the Tottenham franchise, were there to shake hands and wish them well.

From the small crowd of VIPs emerged the sexy, lithe body of Gayle Bingaman, the babe from SportsTime, who liked to conduct naked interviews. She wore a very proper navy blue suit with an impossibly tight, thigh-hugging skirt that stopped five inches above her knees. She had the right kind of body to pour herself into that suit, with the little bit of ruffle showing along the low-cut, frilly blouse looking like it was on the verge of a major clothing malfunction. He didn't understand quite why he was on her radar today, but there was no mistaking he was. He'd seen it happen before, and so he decided to play along. He heard whistles behind him as a way of warning.

Which he hadn't needed.

Her athletic body summoned him almost as if he'd been ensorcelled by some dark angel inside her. His *Veeger*, the childhood nickname he and Ryan had invented for his pecker, was liking the play and stood to attention right on cue. He didn't have a problem with that, either.

"Hello, Patrick." She examined his face for a trace of embarrassment, which he would not give her. Unless he wanted to be harassed for the next ten days while on the team "Friendlies" road trip, he better be stronger than the poor Tottenham Hotspur last year who got his spurs tangled with his tongue and started stuttering. She'd moved on to a bank executive, they were told.

"Hello, Gayle." He cocked his head to see if he could figure her out, searching for any hesitation.

She stared back at him without flinching and then slowly perused the length of his upper torso, as well as the length of the tent in his pants. That's when she finally smiled. To Veeger, she said, "Some days, I just love my job."

Yeah, some days I do, too. I have a fuckin' soccer game to win. Although he suspected her timing was perfect, right now it was going to give him a few problems.

He glanced at his coach, who was having a heart attack, eyes wide and worried his keeper would end up spending the day in the locker room shower or a bathroom stall. Patrick did think about it, but shook himself mentally. They paid him a million dollars a year to chase a little ball around in a box and make sure it didn't score.

But he sure was going to score, just not right now.

The rest of the squad wandered past him. The VIPs got autographs, and mothers sheltered their children and teenage daughters while Patrick invited Gayle into the locker room.

"I thought you'd never ask," she whispered with all the buttered rum she could manage. Her perfume made him sneeze, but her voice made him want to put something inside her mouth. Veeger agreed.

Ronnie, Patrick's roommate on road trips and team best friend, opened the door while whistling a casual tune. This allowed Gayle to sashay her hips into Patrick's thigh. It was a neat trick and got the effect she was obviously looking for.

They stood in the main opposing team locker room, so he nodded in the direction of the training room entrance.

"Why not?" She threw her head back, glanced at everyone who was staring, and at the manager, who was scowling and shaking his head, and then headed toward the labeled door.

"Five minutes," his coach said, holding up his paw with the fingers splayed. "Then I send in Soto and you've got yerself a thousand-dollar fine, Paddy."

"I think this can be wrapped up in five minutes," he said without looking back.

Patrick brought his equipment bag into the little training room. He had to change his shorts from his warmups, so he set his bag on the table and began to get out his gear. She stood about ten inches away while he removed his shirt. Her nostrils flared while she studied him over pretty thoroughly. "I have to get ready while we talk. You don't mind, do you?" He leaned into her, upping the ante, halfway hoping she'd back down. Any second now he expected her to fold or give some kind of nervous laugh, or turn bright red, avoiding eye contact.

She didn't do any of that.

"I don't mind at all. I rather enjoy the view. All of it."

"Really?" Impulsively, he slipped down his warmups and stood in front of her commando-style, Veeger straining forward to touch her. The height difference had him calculating things, angles and hip movements, just like he calculated goal kicks and body language on the field. He started to get more interested in the challenge of this little game.

She thrust the microphone in his face while he attempted to put on his cup and sliding pants. She held the bulbous object like a sex toy. He liked the looks of her fingers wrapped around the silver unit attached to something in her shouldered briefcase.

"Tell me what your thoughts are about the game today."

He squinted at her. "You want it straight or—"

"I like it straight. I don't like to share. There's a time and place to be funny, and this isn't it."

Okay, so she's a ballbuster of the first order. All the rumors about her were totally on target. Veeger was complaining about the cup, the constriction of the sliding pants.

Shut up, Veeger.

"Okay, Miss Gayle. I'm going to fuckin' amaze you." He paused to ask, "Is that thing on?"

"Yes." She wasn't smiling. She was paying rapt attention to his every word.

"I'm going to jump all around the box like a monkey. My arms will be long, my legs and body in full extension to make some incredible saves you're not going to believe."

"Really? I do have quite an active imagination," she whispered.

"I'll bet. We are talking about football now, aren't we?"

He thought for sure she'd eventually flinch, and he'd be let off the hook. Instead, she closed the gap between their upper torsos, brushing her thighs against his, threw the microphone on the table next to his bag and put a lip lock on him with her tongue so deep down his throat he thought she was going to crawl inside. When they parted, she nibbled on his lower lip and rubbed her breasts against his bare chest. "How about we get together after the game, so you can show me some of those moves?"

She had a point.

"Done deal," he heard himself say.

IT WAS ONE of the most difficult games he'd ever played, and of course he did none of the things he'd promised. Their team lost nil to four. The coach briefly reminded them that, just because Paddy hadn't saved them the way he normally did, the lack of scoring on the part of the forwards also contributed to the loss. But Patrick saw the coach was disgusted with him, and he was a little sorry for that.

That's when it hit him. He'd been looking for distraction, because the game didn't call to him anymore. It had been that way for a while now. And he was even beginning to tire of the extracurricular activities, too. Was this all he had to look forward to, and was it enough? He'd loved the game growing up, but now it was just a job without a higher calling.

He wasn't up to a night of calisthenics with Gayle, but his male ego required that if, by some miracle, he was saved from screwing her, he better make the team think otherwise.

Since it was a "Friendly" game, and there would be another the next day, the fact that they'd lost wouldn't affect their standings. But he'd started to get on the coach's bad side, and that was never a good sign. He realized his attitude sucked big time. The poor guy's job was on the line, since coaches didn't have the same contractual protection the players did. All his coach wanted to do was win. And Patrick had just taken away a bargaining chip for the man.

Against his better judgment, he'd arranged for Gayle to meet him at their hotel. His roommate Ronnie had already hooked up with a dark-haired beauty who was taller than he was by a good two inches.

Patrick leaned over and whispered to Ronnie's ear as they entered the hotel lobby, "You'd best ask some questions before you get too far. I think she is a he."

"Oh, shut up, Patrick. She's a bird."

"Just a friendly word of caution."

"She bringing the whole film crew?" Ronnie said as he saw Gayle approach with a cameraman in tow.

"Holy crap," Patrick muttered.

"Bah, you're in for it tonight with that one. Kinda wish I hadn't set all this up. I wanted to get to bed early. You should too."

"Trust me, I will be. So then, you want the room?"

"Yes. You're the one with the seven-figure income. I say you get your own room, Paddy."

"Fair enough."

Gayle was keen to make another attempt to embarrass him on camera, but he stayed cool and aloof.

Maybe she thought he was playing hard to get, but the truth was he was tired and needed a good night's sleep.

She asked him questions about his performance on the field today, which was painful. He lost interest in her in proportion to how much she probed and came onto him. Normally, this kind of play was fun, but tonight, he was just tired. Tired of it all.

"What do you think got you so flustered today?" she asked as she smoothed over his chest. The cameraman had started to follow her hand but then abruptly kept the focus on their faces.

Patrick really didn't like her lack of discretion.

"Sometimes you have good days and sometimes you have bad days. Today was just a bad day," he said with a shrug. "Unlike European players we have in the Premier League, I've played with some of these guys on Seattle's team before, here in the states, and they know my method of play well. I'm guessing the element of surprise was gone."

It was a truthful, or what he hoped would be a truthful, answer. The interview was quickly over.

She nodded at the cameraman, dismissing him.

"Time for a little fun?" She jiggled the contents of her bag, and he heard a lot of metal clanking.

Okay, so much for an early night.

"Gayle, not sure what you had in mind, but I do have to get some rest."

"I promise to let you do that."

"In that case, let me just do one thing first."

He took out his cell while he slipped the key card into the new room door, letting her into the darkened room.

He sent a text to Ronnie,

If I'm not down at breakfast, get an extra key and come untie me. Room 10214.

Satisfied he'd covered all the bases, he entered after her, closing the door behind him.

CHAPTER 2

AS THE ONLY American on the squad, Patrick always got a lot of attention when he played in the United States. He hoped Gayle's short interview with him would get ample exposure, since some of his friends and family watched the games from their homes as often as they could.

The next morning, Patrick sent Gayle off abruptly, and she bristled over being rushed. He'd reached the threshold where he wasn't so sure he'd be doing anonymous hookups any longer. Was it his imagination or were women suddenly going crazy all around him? Where were the normal women? Or, was it just that, in this arena, the normal types were not part of the entourage?

He felt like a big kid, really. Like he'd never grown up from high school. It was always the same; coaches wanting to win. School officials, and now franchise owners, wanted a W on the board at all costs, and the players wanted to do well without being injured. The money was good if you didn't get injured. With no health insurance or benefits to speak of, if you took a career-ending injury, it was back to coaching grade-schoolers or summer soccer camps at universities. He could be watching football, but from the sidelines. He was always one bad injury away from unemployment.

Patrick had been hired before he even finished college, playing in the developmental group for a couple of years until he was moved up as a first-team player five years ago. It was the achievement of his life's goal to play *The Beautiful Game,* as the Brazilians called it. But something had changed. He wasn't quite sure what it was. He still loved to play, but the expected extracurricular activities were beginning to bore him. Was he becoming something he was no longer proud of? He never imagined he'd ever feel this way. It had nothing to do with soccer, either.

Many of the team players had wives and families. Patrick had never been interested in anything permanent…but he also wasn't interested in anything he had to regret the next morning. 'Easy in, easy out' had always been his motto. It had served him well while he and Ryan worked their way through the lovelies in high school, and it was no different now.

He thought about Ryan jumping out of airplanes or helos at night, doing all that crazy shit for less than five percent of the money Patrick made. But Ryan, a Navy SEAL, didn't do it for the money. He was the true patriot, a hero through and through. Patrick was in it for the money—and for the love of the game.

Right out of high school, Ryan had enlisted in the Navy, wanted to be a SEAL even though there'd been no guarantee he could go for the BUD/S training. The day after his eighteenth birthday he was shipped off to the Great Lakes Training Facility—the same week Patrick picked up that full-ride to college. They'd been inseparable since grammar school; they'd played together on every sports team time would allow. But then, while Patrick became the first American goalkeeper on the English squad, Ryan had become a decorated Navy SEAL.

And Ryan had one other thing Patrick had always envied. He had Stephanie.

The two of them used to make fun of her in grammar school, even though the three of them went everywhere together. In middle school and high school, they competed for her attention. Sometimes, the three of them would go to the movies, on those rare occasions when Patrick actually had free time.

When Patrick's training intensified, his absence made it possible for Stephanie and Ryan to grow closer, and that first Christmas Patrick spent in London, Ryan went home on leave and asked Stephanie to marry him.

Stephanie turned him down. Ryan had been inconsolable, but all Patrick could do was run up a five-hundred-dollar phone bill he didn't have the money to pay. His advice, coming all the way from London, was seldom heeded. Patrick had helped Ryan compose letters to Stephanie, counseled him what to say. Eventually, it began to soften her tough veneer, and she had finally agreed to marry Ryan. They had set the wedding date for this fall, just three months away.

Today was a new day, a new game. He'd thought about Ryan all during the first half of the game. He'd made two outstanding saves he was proud of. The coach was beaming. The players, all except the backup keepers, were happy.

At halftime, they were up one-zip. The coach gave them the "most dangerous score for the beautiful game," meaning it was wrong to get overly confident or think the game was won, because the other side would be working overtime to change the odds. If they evened the score, the momentum would definitely be in the opposition's favor.

"Dangerous, gents. We're ahead, and Patrick will work miracles for us. Right Paddy?" The coach liked to bring an arm around his neck, treating as if he'd been raised as the coach's Irish son. Patrick was pleased the antics of the previous day were all but forgotten. "But he needs your help. Even Patrick can't do it all. You show up, or you go home having been beaten by American pussies." The team chuckled, like they always did when he said that. "Later, you can get yourselves some American pussy and play your own games, but tonight, we do what we're known for."

They stood up and cheered, *"To Dare Is to Do."* Their Tottenham Hotspur motto.

A security guard entered their hallowed waiting room while the team re-applied hair gel, re-taped their shin guards, re-tied their shoes, and drank sparse sips of energy drink.

"Got an urgent phone call for Patrick Harrington." The guard scanned the room. Patrick had been listening to a CD Ryan had made for him with some of the workout songs his SEAL Team 5 used, but he heard the booming voice and saw everyone turn toward him. He stood and was ushered out the rear door and down a narrow corridor with a flickering neon light that made him feel like he'd just stepped onto the set of a sci-fi flick.

His cleats were loud. In White Hart, their home stadium, they had carpeting, protecting the shoes that cost the club five hundred dollars a pair, but he tried to be casual about it. Besides, they'd said the call was important, and he didn't have time to unlace and re-tape his shoes.

He was careful on the slippery concrete with his

longer spikes. He'd worn them because they'd overwatered the lawn, as they often did in Seattle. He was breaking in a new pair, since this was a friendly, and their real season would start in three weeks.

The stench of cigarettes hit him when the security office door first opened, revealing several overweight gentlemen in uniform and a pretty blonde wearing a hat way too big for her head.

"Right here, Patrick." She pointed to the handset.

"Hello?"

"Patrick, this is Molly Rosen, Ryan's mom."

"Hey, Mrs. Rosen." He was happy to hear from his best friend's mother, but the call sent a chill down his spine. "Is Ryan okay?"

"No, I'm sorry, but I have some bad news. Ryan was killed the day before yesterday in—I'm not sure how to pronounce the name, but it was somewhere in Afghanistan. He comes home tomorrow."

Ryan was gone? He sat down without being offered the chair. He planted his forehead into his palm.

"Oh, no. Oh, my God. I'm so sorry. I just can't believe it." Patrick's ears began to buzz, and he recognized signs of heightened blood pressure.

"Pat, I hope this isn't imposing, but I read you were in Seattle doing 'Friendlies.' I wonder if your club would give you time off to attend his service? We were hoping you'd speak."

Given how well he'd been playing, he figured the manager might let him off. "Absolutely. I'll request it."

The door burst open, and one of the assistant managers barked that he needed to get back with the team. Patrick gave Mrs. Rosen his cell number.

"Text me your contact information, and I'll ask the manager right after the game. Right now, I have to get back on the field."

SANTA ROSA WAS the county seat, in the heart of Sonoma County's wine country. Their warm summer days and nights meant he'd been able to play outdoor sports year round. A healthy mix of players from Mexico and Central America populated the soccer teams especially, but also baseball.

But Patrick's six-foot-four height and agility made him a natural goalkeeper. He also had the basketball coach bending his parents' ears about playing for him. The football—American football—coach wanted him to be a punter for their high school team. And he held the school record for number of home runs his sophomore year, before he'd had to limit his sports to three, and then two, and then to just soccer because of his heavy training schedule in his senior year.

Ryan elected to play junior varsity in everything but soccer, which always had been his first love, too. Patrick knew part of his desire to stay with soccer had been so they could play together. Ryan was a defender and worked closely with Patrick. Their communication was almost telepathic.

But today, after he picked up his rental car at the airport terminal, the breeze wasn't gentle. It was piercing cold, like his insides. He wondered if the plane bringing Ryan home had already landed. He didn't see the motorcycle escort Ryan's mother had told him would be there.

Hang on there, buddy. I'm coming.

He still couldn't believe Ryan was gone.

Patrick's parents were going to arrive tomorrow, barely in time for the service. They'd retired and moved to Oregon to be close to Patrick's sister and her kids.

He dialed the Rosens and told them where he was staying.

His thoughts drifted off to Stephanie. He'd spent most of his high school nights dreaming about her and then beating himself up about it. He felt guilty for thinking about her now, but she was one of those women who just made him feel happier to be around her. He felt like more of a man. She was uncomplicated and didn't require he play the kind of role other women expected of him.

And she had been devoted to Ryan, which meant she'd be devastated right now. His heart reached out to her, wishing he had her cell. There had been a time he believed he'd had a chance with her, but when Ryan wrote to him, telling him of his intentions, Patrick took two long goalkeeper leaps backward and stayed in the shadows of their relationship. It wasn't hard to do. He was halfway around the world.

He hadn't seen her for two years now. He wondered how she'd make him feel. With equal parts apprehension and anticipation, he hoped she'd be at the Rosens' home tonight. He laid out his shave kit, stared back at himself while mentally talking to Ryan, and began to lather up his face. The shaving soap and boar bristle brush, the only things he'd inherited from his grandfather, went with him everywhere. At first, Ryan had given him a hard time about his "old-fashioned" shaving kit, but then he started to do the same thing, even using the same soap from an English toiletry catalog they both ordered from online.

Miss you already, buddy. I wished we had many more years of friendship.

This was all backwards. For a brief second, he thought he caught a glimpse of Ryan in his reflection, as if his best friend were somewhere behind the looking glass, guiding his hand while he shaved.

CHAPTER 3

WHEN STEPHANIE GOT the news about Ryan, she'd been in shock for a while, and then she found it impossible to concentrate. By mid-afternoon, she finally had to give up trying to make phone calls, took a bath, and then put herself to bed early.

Tonight, she was supposed to go over to the Rosens' house. Her eyes were red and burning. She didn't think she could shed another tear this century. She'd cried so much over the evening, waking up confused, wondering why she felt so bad, and then remembering, which brought on another wave of tears until she cried herself to sleep again.

This pattern had been repeated many times. In the morning, after looking at herself in the mirror, her eyes red and so puffy she could hardly see out of them, she wished it wasn't so important for to greet the guests who would gather tonight at the Rosens' to honor Ryan. But it was her duty, and it affirmed her love and respect for the man she'd been about to marry.

Every time she thought about the finality of his being gone, the tears flowed. She put cool washcloths on her blotchy face and chest and lay down again. The phone had been ringing, but outside of her parents, she didn't want to talk to anyone. She'd made all the calls to former high school friends yesterday. She'd asked for their help in spreading the word. That was all she could do. Thank goodness it was summer vacation at the preschool. Then again, it would be easier if she had something to do other than think about how much she missed Ryan.

Dammit. Here come the tears again.

Early evening fell, and exhausted, she drove over to the Rosens'. She greeted guests, feeling disconnected, the sounds muffled. She was the daughter-in-law-to-be, as opposed to the real daughter-in-law, but her grief was every bit as bad, and so was theirs. But they were not her parents, and Stephanie missed her parents now more than ever.

Everyone at the gathering was a friend of the Rosens, and she didn't see anyone even close to her own age. There were a few of their Jewish relatives. Though Ryan had not been raised in the Jewish tradition, it was part of his family's heritage and was more visible today than she'd remembered. A rabbi would be attending the graveside service tomorrow, as well as the Presbyterian minister who had agreed to marry them. That brought on even more tears.

She could feel Ryan's absence, a yawning, empty place among the nicely dressed and polite company of the elder Rosens. The gathering was catered. She wondered why none of his friends from school showed up. She knew some of the younger crowd planned to attend tomorrow's graveside funeral, at least she hoped so. Everything seemed so rushed, though.

It was silly, but she kept looking for Ryan, who should have been sitting in a chair, nodding in quiet agreement. He had a gentle way about him, listening respectfully when an elder gave him advice, which was more pronounced after he'd made the Teams. She'd loved him before, but as he filled the SEAL uniform and carried out his missions, he got taller, his chest broader, and he stood straighter. He was more patient, and he focused on her and her alone when they were together. She didn't know which Ryan she loved more, the one she'd known her whole life or the man he'd become.

He always had respected his parents and their friends. She'd never heard him speak an ill word about anyone the last couple of years. He was their only son, since Ryan's older brother died as a child. So she kept searching the crowd, between the gnarled hands and kisses to her wet cheeks. She shared tears with people she didn't even know, but she understood their pain, because it was her own. Wrinkled faces with kind smiles and concerned brows spoke softly to her. These were people, they said, who had planned to attend their wedding.

Dang, the tears again.

Like some tragic Shakespearean actress walking across the stage, she was feeling heavy, infected with a kind of sadness pox. If it was a funeral for someone else, she'd be invisible, and how she wished she could be invisible now. She wasn't a bride or a widow. She was the tragic fiancée of a man who had given his life and had left behind, incomplete, all their hopes and dreams. It just wasn't the way it was supposed to be. He was too good a man to be lost to the world forever.

Her own parents had moved to Florida after she entered college. They would fly out next week, but wouldn't be in time for the funeral. While Stephanie understood, she so wished she had someone in her corner. Ryan had always been that someone. Ryan would have known exactly what to do to calm her down. She told herself yesterday she'd be okay, but now she wasn't sure. It was so unfair.

She continued searching as more guests arrived. A small roar developed when a new person arrived in the foyer. Someone very tall, whose head poked up above the large philodendron in the front room. A man with dark brown hair, not gray. Her heart fluttered a bit, almost faltering, reaching for the connection to a kindred spirit, for someone who might understand her. Someone who knew her, who spoke her language. She set her wine glass down, resisting the urge to run, to fling herself into his arms, to bury her face in his chest, and have a good cry.

Patrick.

He was just stepping back from his embrace with Mrs. Rosen, and her friends were standing around, giving him appreciative glances, with nodding faces, hands clasped together, and the titter of nervous laughter. As he uncoiled from the respectful bear hug and his eyes lifted, she could see the blue-green hue she used to dream about when she wondered as a young girl if it was possible to marry two men and still be a good girl. Later, they'd all talked about it, laughed about it. Ryan had gotten quiet afterward several times. When she'd agreed to marry him, he questioned her about her feelings, her decision to marry him after so many refusals. He was right about one thing. A tiny piece of her had never stopped loving Patrick.

"Hey, Sis," he said, bringing up his favorite nickname for her.

"Hey, Bro," she answered back. It was as close to the secret handshake as any two long-term friends could have.

"I didn't know Stephanie was your sister, Patrick," one of Mrs. Rosen's friends said.

Patrick appraised her respectfully and then said in that proud way only he could do, "In every way but blood, Cici." He tore his eyes off Stephanie to make the point to the older woman, but soon, he was scanning Stephanie's face again, intensely. She felt the unaltered attraction there in her belly again, just like when they played co-ed soccer in grade school and he'd tackle her and then help her up and ask carefully if she'd been hurt.

"You can't hurt me, Patrick," she'd always said, to prove how tough she was, kicking a lump of muddy grass from her cleats. He would look at her and grin, just like he was doing right now.

Mrs. Rosen led her bevy of friends from the foyer and left Patrick and Stephanie alone.

She let him see her breaking heart, her tears, the quiver of her lower lip, the way her chest heaved when she tried to stifle a sob. She was still being the brave little soccer player, and the protection he'd given her when he tempered his tackles on the field waited. He was the tall tree she needed to lose herself in. Unaware of who moved first, they were in each other's arms.

And, dammit, was she losing her mind? She could smell Ryan.

AFTER THE FINAL farewells were said, she overheard Patrick and Mr. Rosen discuss details of the funeral the next day. Then he joined her and walked out the front door to a warm Sonoma County night. She headed toward her car. It jolted her when he put his arm on her shoulder and pulled her to his side. "How you holding up, Stephanie?" he asked in a whisper, facing the traffic in front of them.

"Oh…" And then she sighed, taking another deep breath, trying to quell her tears yet again. "This has been such a shock. Day before yesterday was his last day…" She wrapped her arms around his waist and released the restraint she'd been holding onto for the past hour, sobbing into his shirt.

He was so tall he had to bend down to kiss the top of her head. His long fingers massaged the back of her skull and sifted through her hair, rubbing her scalp in small circles. "Just let it all go, Steph. Get it all out of your system." His warm, buttery voice was such a pleasant and familiar thing, like a child's favorite blanket or stuffed toy.

"I just…can't…believe…he's gone," she sobbed.

"I know. Me, too. Talked to him that morning. It was nighttime there."

"God, I hope he didn't suffer," she said between sobs.

She could tell he wanted to say something but held

back. Instead, he squeezed her harder. "It's going to be okay, Steph. You're strong. You're a strong woman."

"Right now, I don't feel very strong. Now I wish I hadn't made him wait so long. Patrick, he wanted to get married last time he was home. I told him no. I didn't want a…" She couldn't finish.

"Shhhh. Now you're talking gibberish. No way we can change the past. You have to live for the future, Steph. He'd want you to do that. He'd want both of us to do that."

He was right, of course. She didn't know why, but she blurted out something she immediately regretted. "You smell like him. Sort of."

Patrick flinched, but covered it up quickly. "I know you miss him, Sis." He steered her around a large hedge.

"I kept looking for him all evening, like he'd just appear, walk with you in the front door. I expect to see him still. I just can't…"

And then his mouth was on hers. He didn't push, but fed her a gentle kiss, a touch of passion to remind her she was in the present and not in her dreams or in the past. It worked, too. Her thoughts immediately shifted. The scent of him was familiar, even though the taste of him was new. In spite of her grief, she felt her bones unthaw. Her excitement heightened in a non-sexual way, and she gave herself to the kiss before logic began a steady pounding on the door she mistook for her own heartbeat.

What am I doing?

As quickly as it had happened, she pulled away, breathless, needing to see something in his eyes that wasn't pity or pain. She soon confirmed it had not been a sympathy kiss. His eyes sparkled with lust, focused on needing another taste of her. He licked his lips and leaned forward again, but she ducked back this time. He was telling her in the only way she'd understand that she was alive and not ready to be buried in the coffin with Ryan tomorrow morning. He wanted more of what she could give him, and he'd give her what he could in return.

"Forgive me, Steph. I couldn't help it."

"Neither could I." Thank God he didn't call her 'Sis.' She became self-conscious about the people leaving the Rosen home and was grateful for the small amount of cover the landscaping provided. What would they think if they could see the two of them kissing?

"It was good to see you, Patrick. I wish it were under different circumstances." Then she remembered when she had planned to see him again—at her wedding. The tears threatened to spill out over her still-puffy lower lids.

With the softest touch, he raised her chin and

spoke. "Hey, Steph. I'm here for you. Call me tonight if you want to talk."

"No. I'm going to try to get some sleep. I'm exhausted, and I think maybe tonight I can. Thanks, though. I have to buck up for tomorrow, and then I can collapse."

He nodded, and she wanted to ask him, *If I do collapse, would you pick up the pieces?* But she was too tired to have that conversation right now. He stood motionless while she got into her car and pulled away. Watching him in the rear-view mirror, standing there in the moonlight, his image getting smaller and smaller, she started to cry all over again, like she'd lost him, too.

She couldn't trust herself to have a coherent thought.

After all, she was the grieving almost-bride-nearly-widow-kissing-her-fiancé's-best-friend.

Which meant she had completely lost her footing.

CHAPTER 4

PATRICK CURSED HIMSELF all the way back to his hotel. He was second-guessing every decision he'd made since learning Ryan was gone. He shouldn't have been at the Rosens'. He shouldn't have left so early and certainly not with her. He shouldn't have kissed her.

Grief was getting to him. In his haste to put the pain of losing his best friend on ice, he'd reached for something comfortable. Instead of running from pain, he was hiding behind pleasure. His bad habits on the team had spilled over into the wholesome parts of his life, the parts he wanted to protect, not abuse or take advantage of.

Stephanie wasn't like those girls who hung around the stadium and haunted their hotels. Had he lost his good manners? His sanity? She was the gold standard.

No fucking way should he have anything to do with her, regardless of the messages he was getting. He had to keep a straight head. He had to get rid of the tent in his pants. He needed to forget about all the fantasies he had about her growing up, fantasies which had picked this incredibly inappropriate moment to bloom again, just below his belt.

Too late for a workout, since the hotel gym was closed, he decided he'd sneak into the closed pool for a swim. He dove in, traveled the length of the pool underwater before surfacing to take long breaststrokes. He preferred this anyway. It would physically tax him more than anything else he could do. Most days after a game, he would tire easily, but tonight he felt like he could swim forever. He let his mind wander, wondering if he should have tried out for the swim team rather than play soccer. Rather than baseball. Rather than basketball or place-kicking at football.

When he and Ryan had started swimming in grammar school, Ryan had made the team, and Patrick had not. The Guppy program was his first defeat. He'd vowed to never again fail to make the cut, and he'd kept that promise.

Ryan had been a fish. But more than that, he was a natural athlete, succeeding at everything he did. Gymnastics could have been his sport, but he stuck with Patrick—hitting, dribbling or kicking a ball. Only team sports. That meant they could play together.

Just not possible that he was gone. That Stephanie was all alone. He wasn't going to be the man in her life the way Ryan had been, but he wanted to help her get back on her feet. Help her with the numbing cold he knew she must be feeling. But that kiss had not only lit her flame, it had done a pretty damn good job of lighting a bonfire under his ass, too. That had been totally unexpected.

He'd maintained his friendships over the years, players he confided in who'd been traded or gotten injured, and had to leave The Beautiful Game. He made friends easily, and the shared experience of being expendable or only as good as your last game made fellows of complete strangers who came from places he would never visit or even know much about. They had their own kind of brotherhood. Playing on a team meant not letting your mates down, stepping up to the plate when a buddy was having a bad day, covering for a defender who missed something he shouldn't have, and not making a public display when someone's sliding tackle missed or they lost possession of the ball, or when the communication just plain broke down.

He knew this happened to the SEALs overseas. He'd talked about it with Ryan the last time they were together. The only difference was that Ryan admitted he'd die for his brothers. Willingly die. Patrick couldn't see that as something that made much sense, but he respected his buddy's decision, and honored it. But damn, the cost was too great, the price too high.

"So, you think she'll say yes, Patrick?" Ryan had asked him Christmas two years ago.

"Of course, she will," he'd replied. "She'd be a fuckin' nut case if she ever turned you down. And then that would mean the dregs, guys like me, might have a chance."

Ryan played with the towel around his neck that day while they sat in the sauna after a workout. His bright white smile nearly glowed inside the steam-filled and darkened room. "Was a time I thought she was hot for you." Ryan didn't look at him, like he didn't want to see anything in his friend's eyes he couldn't live with.

"Well, if that was the case, it was only so she could get close to you, my friend. She's fuckin' crazy about you, Ryan. She wants your babies. I just know she does."

That had finally made him smile. "Yeah, I want her fuckin' babies, too. I want to get pooped on and spit up on and shit like that. I'd do anything for that little lady. I'd give up anything to have her."

Patrick couldn't tell Ryan then that he was so filled with envy it interfered with their friendship. He told himself he was happy for his friends. He told himself the way she used to look at him was just what young girls did when they don't know how to control all those hormones. It had nothing to do with him. It had everything to do with just plain growing up.

There had been that middle school dance. Ryan was sick with a cold, so, instead of the three of them going together, Patrick had his mom drive him and Stephanie to the dance. He was so nervous that he split off soon as they entered the gym, found a shadowed corner, and tried to stay invisible, watching her turn around and around, searching for him. He watched her dance with few other boys, and then she'd turn and scan the room again.

He'd had to take a piss, so he slipped out the side door. Before he could make it to the boys' bathroom she called out to him.

He looked up at the sky and swore to himself. He was in serious danger of wetting his pants. She was making him hard, and he had to take a pee at the same time, so now he had to worry about that too.

"Patrick, you're hiding from me." It sounded so stupid when she said it. Why would he go and do something like that? Her pink lips glowed under the light of the moon. Her breasts were just starting to develop, and he didn't think she wore a bra yet, because everything was perky, just sticking straight out, like trying to make him fondle them. He was afraid she'd catch him staring at her chest, so he winced, dropping his eyes from the heavens, and tried to look into her face.

Except he looked right at her little perky tits. Again.

"I'm not hiding from you, Sis." Maybe if he called her that, reminded her they were just good friends, maybe then she wouldn't stand so close to him.

"Then why are you frowning? And what is going on with your hands. Are you rubbing yourself?"

Fuckin' yes, he was rubbing himself because he was so hard, which didn't usually happen around live girls, just the ones in the XXX movie houses he and Ryan tried to sneak into. So first she'd called him out on hiding from her, and then she pointed out his inappropriate behavior with his fuckin' Voyager. That was the nickname he and Ryan gave their dicks, from the Star Trek movie. They lovingly called it *veeger*. They'd imagined that actress giving them a blow job, and they laughed at how it made them want to spurt.

But none of that was helping him right then.

Stephanie stepped to close the gap between them. Her wide brown eyes looked up at his face. They weren't as far apart in height they would later be, but she reached up and put her hand on his cheek and said in her innocence, "Kiss me, Patrick. Do it with your tongue. I want to feel that. Can you do it for me?"

With my tongue? Holy fuck, who does that?

But of course, he couldn't say that. He didn't understand how it could feel good. Not at all. He wondered if he'd brushed his teeth. He was sure he hadn't flossed. Was his deodorant working? And what about that fuckin' Willy in his pants?

Veeger was bouncing in avid anticipation, and it made his balls buzz. Things were going off in all directions. Alarms were sounding. He thought he might pee and fart at the same time.

But then he looked at her. She licked those full pink lips and watched as he couldn't help himself and did the same. Next he knew, he was tasting her cherry lip gloss and loving it. She'd opened her mouth, like she expected him to put his tongue inside, and then they heard the catcalls from one of the other boys on his baseball team.

Looking back on those years now, Patrick would have to say that he'd been obsessed with her, and the more Ryan seemed to lean in her direction, the more he was losing her, the more he wanted her.

When they were in grade school, they used to go hiking up in Annadel State Park, swim in the lake, and rest by the water's edge, the three of them holding hands, Stephanie always in the middle. The sky was so blue, and the clouds all funny clown shapes. Later, those shapes would look like ladies' private parts. When he and Ryan had secretly discussed it, Steph always wanted to know what they'd been giggling over, but they never told her.

She was the best part about summer time, being

out of school. She could ride a bike as fast as he could, at least until they got to middle school. She played soccer like a boy, which he kept telling her was a compliment.

He and Ryan would defend her honor if the girls in class got mean with her. He knew most of the girls in the class were jealous that she had not only one handsome boy's attention; she had two. He knew her favorite ice cream, her favorite TV program, and her favorite music. He got to thinking he knew what she was feeling on some of those long summer days when the sun lasted forever and kids stayed outside to play in the street after dinner until dark.

If he could, he would roll back the clock. He'd talk Ryan out of going for the Teams. He might even get bolder with Stephanie. So much might have changed if he had it to do all over again.

But that was folly. The reality was that Ryan was gone. He'd be buried tomorrow. He and Stephanie shared a common pain, hers more painful than his, but she wasn't going to be his girl, and never was.

She was still Ryan's.

And Stephanie would just have to work all that out as best she could, and he'd stand by to protect her, but not take on the role of the leading man. That role had already been taken.

CHAPTER 5

Flowers covered the grave site. Stephanie had never seen so many. The somber crowd of mostly older people—friends of Ryan's parents and parents of their friends growing up. Many of the kids they'd gone to high school with were scattered all over the world, so she recognized only a few.

She stood up front, next to Mr. and Mrs. Rosen. She missed her mom and dad. The vacant spot next to her was filled instead by Patrick's hulking presence. Though she didn't look at him, he slipped his hand in hers like they used to do in grammar school. Their fingers didn't entwine like they did when Ryan always took her hand, but her palm pressed against his, and she could feel the pulse of the underside of his wrist as their forearms touched.

On the other side of the coffin stood several uniformed SEALs, presumably all friends of Ryan's. They were different heights and sizes, but all wore identical black wraparound sunglasses, spoke little, didn't smile, and had square, sober jawlines.

After the opening hymn, they were instructed to be seated. During the short sermon, she thought about Ryan and the things she would miss the most about him—the little mischievous smile he got when he was going to do something she didn't expect. The flowers he liked to bring her on the spur of the moment. How he loved puppies and always stopped to pet them, no matter where they were or how late they were going to be. How he loved the children and how they loved him when he stopped by the preschool to pick her up for lunch. She remembered the tenderhearted letters he'd written her from places she had no desire to ever see.

The words of the pastor droned on in the background as she said her private farewell to the man she thought she'd spend the rest of her life with. She was relieved that her tears, at least for now, seemed to be under control.

She examined the SEALs, this time more carefully. One by one, she was acknowledged with a slight nod of the head, something probably no one else in the crowd would recognize. She sucked in air, bracing herself for an outburst of tears, until Patrick squeezed her hand. She wondered how many of these gatherings Ryan had attended. How many other fiancées and wives had to sit and listen to the final words delivered about a life not yet fully begun. She and Ryan had never talked about this, about death or what could happen to a man on the Teams. Like it was bad luck to do so.

At first, Stephanie thought Patrick had dropped her hand because he somehow felt self-conscious that they were showing affection for one another in front of these SEALs. But then she saw the clergyman nod in Patrick's direction. He stood then, perhaps the tallest person in the crowd, his black jacket hanging from his straight shoulders when he turned and faced Ryan's coffin in front of him.

"Ryan and I were friends before I understood what that meant or what a gift it was," he began. "He was always there. My first memories of staying out late and playing in the street until our parents dragged us in were with Ryan."

Stephanie remembered those hot summer nights that seemed to go on forever, hating to leave the childhood games in the streets in front of her house, being so excited to be alive it was hard to sleep.

He glanced up at Stephanie, and her heart clenched in her chest. "And then there was Stephanie. After that, it was the three of us. Inseparable." His voice trailed off when he studied her face then smiled, looking at his feet.

Stephanie peered over at the crowd. The SEALs were all focused on this tall best friend who had been such an important part of Ryan's childhood. A couple of them glanced back at her and watched as Patrick's words filled the garden area of the cemetery.

"I couldn't imagine playing on a team without Ryan there right beside me. It took me a while to get used to it, actually, when I first played in Europe, like I'd expect him to just come onto the field and make some half-assed—" he glanced at Mrs. Rosen who was watching with rapt attention, a Kleenex poised at her nose—"sorry, ma'am. I just expected he'd walk on the field and touch the ball, send it clear out of the stadium somewhere. I expect to see him show up here and just hold court, laugh at all of us all dressed up on his behalf."

A gentle rolling chuckle filtered through the crowd.

Patrick's shoulders dropped when he sighed. "He was the best friend a boy, or a man, could ever want. If you were going to get into trouble, Ryan was the guy you'd want to get sent to the principal's office with. He had the craziest ideas for dumb stuff we used to do all the time. I never could outdrink him, and believe me, I tried."

Again, a rolling chuckle came from the audience.

"We didn't see much of each other during the past five years or so after I went off to play in Europe," Patrick smiled down on the casket, "as I attempted to perfect my drinking and womanizing skills." He sobered, and lowered his voice, "And I saw with my own eyes how Ryan became the man he became. Upright and strong. Couldn't believe the change in him. Last time I saw him, we didn't drink so much—well, *he* didn't anyway."

The audience responded again. Stephanie saw Patrick flick a tear from his left eye with his forefinger.

"While I was touring Europe and getting to know the men on my team, men from all over the world, he played in *his* arena, with a *new* team." He nodded to the SEALs who stood, expressionless.

"He loved his life. He loved what he did. He told me once he felt lucky to have figured out what he'd always wanted to do with his life." As his blue eyes penetrated the fragile shell of Stephanie's demeanor, she felt herself melt into him as he added, "And the woman he wanted to spend it with."

She felt the brief touch of their lips from last night and the memory of his breath on her face, when he whispered to her intimately, but in front of everyone, "I'm sorry."

Mrs. Rosen lost it then, sobbing into her husband's chest, being consoled by several friends behind her as Patrick made his way to Stephanie's side, sat down, and took her hand again.

Stephanie couldn't look at him, so she whispered to their entwined fingers, which now rested on his thigh.

"Thank you. That was beautiful."

The rabbi began his long lament, in lilting voice, a shawl draped over his head. Several others in the audience covered their heads as well. He stopped for the audience response, which was repeated several times.

At the end of the service, the pastor motioned to one of the SEALs to come forward, a tall man who held his white cap under his arm. With deliberate but somehow delicate movements, he removed his sunglasses and pulled out a folded white sheet of paper. What he read touched her heart.

"In times of war or uncertainty there is a special breed of warrior ready to answer our Nation's call. A common man with uncommon desire to succeed. Forged by adversity, he stands alongside America's finest special operations forces to serve his country, the American people, and protect their way of life. I am that man.

My Trident is a symbol of honor and heritage. Bestowed upon me by the heroes that have gone before, it embodies the trust of those I have sworn to protect. By wearing the Trident I accept the responsibility of my chosen profession and way of life. It is a privilege that I must earn every day.

My loyalty to Country and Team is beyond

reproach. I humbly serve as a guardian to my fellow Americans always ready to defend those who are unable to defend themselves. I do not advertise the nature of my work, nor seek recognition for my actions. I voluntarily accept the inherent hazards of my profession, placing the welfare and security of others before my own.

I serve with honor on and off the battlefield. The ability to control my emotions and my actions, regardless of circumstance, sets me apart from other men. Uncompromising integrity is my standard. My character and honor are steadfast. My word is my bond.

We expect to lead and be led. In the absence of orders I will take charge, lead my teammates and accomplish the mission. I lead by example in all situations.

I will never quit. I persevere and thrive on adversity. My Nation expects me to be physically harder and mentally stronger than my enemies. If knocked down, I will get back up, every time. I will draw on every remaining ounce of strength to protect my teammates and to accomplish our mission. I am never out of the fight.

We demand discipline. We expect innovation. The lives of my teammates and the success of our mission depend on me – my technical skill, tactical proficiency, and attention to detail. My training is never complete.

We train for war and fight to win. I stand ready to bring the full spectrum of combat power to bear in order to achieve my mission and the goals established by my country. The execution of my duties will be swift and violent when required yet guided by the very principles that I serve to defend.

Brave men have fought and died building the proud tradition and feared reputation that I am bound to uphold. In the worst of conditions, the legacy of my teammates steadies my resolve and silently guides my every deed. I will not fail."

The big SEAL inhaled, staring down at Ryan's casket, and shouted, "Petty Officer Ryan!"

The crowd of SEALs to his left stood and shouted the return, "Hooyah, Petty Officer Ryan!"

The service was concluded with the pounding of over twenty Tridents into the casket, one by one. Some pressed their emblem into the wood; some punched it down with a fist. All of them had their public and private moment with Ryan in a sendoff she would never forget. One green-uniformed soldier pressed a spear patch onto the casket, since he didn't have a gold Trident.

It took a few seconds for her to fully realize the finality of the Trident ceremony. This was the end of things and the beginning of the rest of her life. She wavered a bit, and Patrick was there to steady her. The Rosens grabbed her, and she was hugged and held by many of their older friends. When she was left alone at last, Patrick had hung back, away from the casket, in the shadows. She sought him out.

"Shall we say goodbye to him together?" she asked.

"Can't do that, Steph. Just can't. Is that wrong?"

"Not at all," she said, as naturally as it was to slip her hand inside his and squeeze. "Not at all. He would totally understand." After Patrick met her gaze, she added. "I understand. But I have to do it."

"Go ahead. I'll wait for you."

He was looking at someone standing behind her. It was the tall SEAL who had read the excerpt at the funeral.

"Ma'am," he said and cleared his throat. "I'm Trevor Markham, and I was Ryan's LPO, his platoon leader." He extended his hand, which she shook. Several of the other SEALs came up behind Trevor and closed ranks around both her and Patrick. "Ryan requested I be present in case—" He winced and looked up to Patrick. "It was his wish. The rest of the team is still in Djibouti. Anyway, Ryan spoke of you often, and I want you to know it was our honor to serve with him. He saved some lives that day, some of them our teammates, who unfortunately could not be here today. I just wanted you to know that, ma'am. He died a hero, not that it makes it any easier. But it's my honor and duty to let you know."

His brief speech, delivered flawlessly and with quiet confidence, struck her as being one of the things she'd loved about Ryan, who had become more a man while his training prepared him for overseas duty. She'd noticed and appreciated his changes, at first looking for something she wouldn't be able to handle, and finally believing that the longer he was involved with his Team buddies, the more he loved them, the more completely he loved her as well. He'd gone into the Navy a young man and graduated a man's man—and a man a woman could love even more deeply.

"Thank you. I wish I could say the same, Trevor. He didn't speak much of you guys, except little tidbits here and there. Stupid things, really," she replied.

That got a chuckle from several of the other SEALs.

"Yeah. That would be Ryan." He extended his hand again. "You need anything, let us know. We'll look in on you if you want. Anytime you want to talk, you just let me know, okay?"

"Thank you," she said, holding the card he had given her. "I appreciate this. Ryan would appreciate this."

One by one, she shook hands with the men and then stood beside Patrick, watching them walk across the lawn to two black waiting Hummers.

"I got some place I want to take you, Steph, if you don't mind."

"Give me a moment, Patrick. Just a moment, okay?"

"Sure, Steph."

She walked to Ryan's flower-draped casket and let her tears trickle gently down her cheeks. "I am so sorry, my love. I will love you forever. I will miss you forever. I will grieve for you forever. This was not the dream I had for us, Ryan. This was not supposed to happen this way, not to us. Never to us." She bent over, suddenly overcome, and then Patrick was there, helping her stand with a big arm around her waist. As she leaned into him, she wiped her wet cheeks with the backs of her hands. He said something to the top of her head she did not understand.

"Goodbye, Ryan." She had to turn and bury her face in Patrick's shirt and jacket, crying uncontrollably. "Why, Patrick? Why did this happen?"

"We don't know why, honey."

"It's so not fair."

"No, it's not. But it is what it is." After a pause, he whispered, "Ready?"

She nodded.

Not only didn't she mind that he was leading her away from the gravesite, she almost wanted to run away from it, away from this place of final rest. She'd done everything she was supposed to do. The controlled demeanor and quiet weeping was over. She was tired. She wanted to relax, get away from crowds, get her mind off the sight of green lawn and marble headstones.

"Where are we going?"

"Oh, I think you'll recognize it," he said, slipping his arm around her waist again.

"I'm supposed to go over to the Rosens'. Aren't you coming?"

"Yes. Then I'm meeting up with the SEALs later tonight."

"Why don't we just make a brief appearance first? I'd like it if you were there, too. I don't want to face everyone again alone."

"Sure. Let's drop your car off at your place, and then I'll drive you."

"Okay. You can follow me."

"Fair enough." He walked by her side, this time not holding her hand. She was grateful for the distance. She was grateful he was not going to leave her side until she was safely home and she could finally collapse in private.

CHAPTER 6

THEY LEFT THE Rosens' house just when the orange sun was beginning to dip low in the July sky. It wasn't yet dusk, but the late afternoon glow bathed everything in golden light. Patrick drove them to their old grammar school, set among mature trees he remembered as being saplings back when they attended classes here. He took her hand and led her across the playground, now abandoned, but he could almost hear the roar of the crowd of children who used to surround them.

He cradled Stephanie's hand, holding it at his back. Behind him was the same little girl he used to dream about when he first knew it was a good thing to want to be part of a friendship. Now it was just the two of them, not the three of them. The triangle had been forever altered, but he knew it still existed somewhere in the back of Stephanie's mind. Patrick had no problem accepting that.

He took a seat on the low wooden table with the attached bench seats and dropped her hand. "You are probably wondering why I brought you here." He smiled at the amused look on her face, which was exactly what he wanted to see.

She looked around the playground and nodded. "Ryan and I were sitting right there." He pointed to the bench seat behind him. And then he angled his forefinger toward the darkened entrance to the classrooms. "He told me there was a new girl, the most beautiful girl I would ever see, and that she'd walk out that door in a minute, carrying a pink lunch box."

He watched her turn and examine the hallway, blushing. Could she remember that day? Did it affect her the way it had affected him back then? Did her heart lurch? Did she almost lose her breath when they saw each other for the first time?

Time suspended as he gazed at her honey brown hair, the curls that blew slightly in the breeze, just close enough for his fingers to touch them, if he dared, and yes, close enough that he could smell her perfume and the fragrance of her shampoo. He felt an overwhelming urge to protect her from harm, help her deal with the pain. At the same time, he was smart enough to know that with the renewed intensity of his feelings for her, it would be totally unwise to reveal it.

I will know, Stephanie, if we have a chance if I can

see it in your eyes. The next few seconds will tell me everything I ever wanted to know.

He waited for her. Waited for her to think about what he'd said. Someday, maybe he'd be able to tell her that he'd thought about no one else. Forever, all women would be compared to Stephanie. Why hadn't he recognized it sooner?

Oh yeah. That's because she's been Ryan's girl.

He'd remembered her walking out, lunch box in her hand, squinting in the late morning sun, hand shading her eyes, looking for a place to sit. And then their eyes had locked. His six-year-old body sat straight up, and he must have given her a toothless smile, because she came right over. Like it was destined.

And here they were again.

The fact that she didn't turn around right away meant she was thinking about something. With her back to him still, facing the darkened hallway, she nodded.

Was she thinking about Ryan? Is that why she didn't turn? Did it matter?

"I remember that day, Patrick," she said, still looking straight ahead. Then she did something miraculous. Turning, she told him something he'd hoped was true, had dreamed about for years. "You were the one I was walking to. I hadn't even seen Ryan. I was coming to you."

Their eyes met without shame. She wasn't blushing, and for the moment, she wasn't crying. He'd never looked at her this honestly before, not as a man. His body responded like it always did when he was around beautiful women, but he did not act on his urge. He waited again. He didn't want to push.

"Funny how you remember some things and then not others. Like I don't remember the first time I met Ryan. He was just always there. But you, Patrick, I remember that day."

He was thrilled.

"I liked your freckles. And do you remember, you brushed the bench before I sat down?"

He hadn't remembered that part. Shaking his head, he answered, "Only thing I remember was you and that pink lunch box. I think you had on a pink sweater, too."

"I wore more pink than anything else. It was my 'neutral color' back then."

Patrick remembered that. He and Ryan used to call her Princess Pink. He decided not to tell her that, just yet.

"Why did you bring me here?"

Patrick shrugged. "I just wanted you to know, that's all. I wanted you to know that the day I met you, it was special. Always has been special."

She immediately dropped her eyes and swung her

body from side to side. He saw her chew on the lower lip he wanted to kiss so badly. She examined her forearms, watching them as her hands reached up to his chest, where she laid her palms on his pecs. She didn't press. The warmth from her hands infused him with delicious heat which traveled up his neck. She slid her fingers to the sides and felt his muscles, kneading his shoulders and then squeezing his biceps, sliding her hands down to the crooks of his elbows.

He allowed his fingers to press the small of her back very lightly, pulling her closer.

But then she abruptly dropped her hands and stepped back. "I can't do this," she whispered, her cheeks flushed, sounding out of breath.

He was horribly disappointed, but knew he had no choice but to appear gracious. "Fair enough," he replied softly, but his voice broke. "Just know that I am here. I've always been here for you, Stephanie."

She nodded at the ground, her arms folded in front of her. "I think I want you to take me home now, please."

"No problem, Steph." He stood and stretched his long legs and arms like he was warming up in the box. "It's been a long day, and you must be exhausted. Come on."

He put his hand up to the back of her neck, and at first he felt her jerk, clearly uncomfortable with the intimate gesture. He made a mental note to stay *completely* away from any physical touching that could be construed as sexual in nature. He didn't want to make her feel uneasy. He was starting to beat himself up about it on the way to his car when she took his hand, stopped him, and said, "Patrick, thank you. I have a lot to sort out, but thank you for being my friend." Her forlorn face was utterly kissable.

"No problem."

"I'm a mess inside, and I don't think I can be anyone's friend until I figure that out first. But I will. I always do."

He knew that about her. She played in the street so hard her braids were always coming undone, her face often streaked with dirt. But he didn't care. He'd thought she was the most beautiful girl in the whole world.

And he'd never stopped thinking it.

CHAPTER 7

First Class Petty Officer Trevor Markham had invited Patrick to join them for drinks and dinner at the Mexican restaurant near their hotel. He was laughing about something one of the other men had said. There was a trail of longneck beer bottles snaking their way back and forth across the table. Patrick wondered why they didn't just buy a pitcher and save some money.

"Hey there, Patrick. Come, we got your seat right here."

Room was made for him on one of the benches next to LPO Markham. Before he could ask, he was handed a bottle of beer, and the salute went up. "Hooyah, Ryan," they chorused.

Quiet ensued when they guzzled their brews. Patrick considered the impact that downing a full bottle on an empty stomach might have on him, and his ability to get back to the hotel.

"So, what's it like playing soccer in England, son?" Markham asked. He was perhaps five years Patrick's senior, so the term struck him as odd.

"It's fun. One of the best jobs in the world."

"What do you like about it?" one of the other SEALs asked.

"Get to train outdoors. I have all this cool equipment and gear. They bus us all around Europe, fly us to South America and places like that. Lots of girls, and the money's good."

"Well," Markham said after he'd finished off his longneck, "up until the part about the money, I thought you were talking about our little club."

Several other men chuckled, and then someone swore and followed it up with, "Ain't that the truth?"

"But the equipment is better," said a young man with a southern accent.

"A whole lot more dangerous, too," Patrick said.

"I've seen those pictures of fans tipping over buses in Brazil, some ref getting beaten to death over a call. I'd say your line of work can be dangerous."

"Yes, we get some defender coming at my head with his cleats up, I could lose an eye or get scarred. But heck, I got scars all over my body, and it doesn't make a bit of difference."

"Shit, I got run through with a crowbar-type tool some months back," the southern boy drawled. He lifted his shirt and showed Patrick a pink scar that looked like bubble gum stuck to the right side of his navel. "Goes clear through to the other side," he said as he attempted to turn around and show him.

That started a whole round of scar reveals. One SEAL was missing an earlobe from hand-to-hand combat. Most of them had more tattoos than scars, so after they'd run out of scars, they started showing them off. Patrick saw some beautiful, intricate designs. He knew Ryan had a bone frog with a trident on his chest right over his heart, and he suspected these men all did as well.

"You been playing a long time?" Markham asked.

"Yessir. Started playing professional just after high school and am now First Squad for Tottenham. It's a good club. A good gig."

"Yeah, Ryan mentioned that. He talked a lot about you, Patrick."

He looked between the faces of these powerful-looking, straight-shouldered men with quiet countenances, noticed how they observed people without staring, how comfortable they were with each other. He listened to their banter and smack talk, but they all remained respectful of his friendship with Ryan, careful not to tread on any of his feelings. He liked them. There was the bond between them that he envied. It was more than the bond he had with the international crowd he played soccer with.

He found himself asking questions. He got half-answers, usually followed up with a smile, leaving the door open for him to ask another probing question, which was not always answered, either. What he liked best about them was that their egos were definitely present, but not dropped on the table naked or allowed to roam around without diapers. The "diapers" comment was one of his favorite expressions, invented by his defender friend Ronnie, who hated drama yet had gotten into so many fights he had a perpetually broken nose. He wore white tape over his nose more days than he didn't of late.

They need to wear diapers, mate.

It was Ronnie's way of saying someone wasn't discreet or was raging like a woman—which, in Ronnie's case, was the worst behavior a man could exhibit. He smiled, thinking about Ronnie, who would be leaving the team next year to play rugby.

Because I'm rotting, Paddy. All rotting footballers in England go play rugby, he'd said.

The SEALs were cautious, not boastful and seeking attention like The Beautiful Game football players were known for in Brazil. These warriors did things with measured and calculated determination. They liked to have fun in a big way, similar to his Tottenham teammates, but it was a private, quiet kind of fun, without drawing attention to themselves, with less public intoxication and spectacle, the kind of rowdy behavior which was privately encouraged in the soccer clubs.

Markham wrinkled his forehead and sucked in his lower lip with a scowl. "What's the deal with Ryan's ex?"

That's an excellent question.

"Why don't you ask her yourself?" Patrick replied and stared back hard.

"I intend to, don't worry. I intend to," the SEAL said as he looked outside the bar to observe cars driving past the open doors of the restaurant. "But with you being Ryan's best friend, I kinda noticed that you might be sweet on her yourself."

It didn't take a genius to figure that out. She was beautiful. He'd known her for a long time. She needed consoling, and she was obviously now unattached, not that it held any promise for anyone at the table this evening.

Patrick felt like there was some unwritten code that another SEAL would be trying very hard to take Ryan's place, and if Patrick wanted a shot at her, he'd have to act quickly and decisively. He could say something to dissuade the SEAL Petty Officer.

"We three grew up together. She used to think she could marry both of us, before her parents sat her down and told her how it was in real life. We were pretty close until I left to go play in Europe and Ryan left for his SEAL training."

Markham was one cool cowboy, Patrick could see. "I get your drift, and if you should leave and go back to England, the lady might be in need of another replacement, no offense."

"None taken. Doubt you'll get very far with her, either."

"Ah!" Markham gasped. "One of those?"

Patrick had no idea what he meant, so he shrugged.

"Means she shot you down already," a Latino-looking SEAL ventured.

At that, he had to laugh. "Yeah, I think it would be fair to say that. Not sure how long the waterworks will be running without a plumber. She's asked for, and I'm going to give her, time. And I don't like the idea that you horny frogs would be hanging around to serenade her." He cleared his throat. "No offense intended."

"Or taken," Markham replied.

And that was that. They didn't challenge him. Instead, they told him they'd play fair, and he somehow knew he could count on that. But if he left her alone for an extra-long period of time, the story could change quickly.

He drove away from the gathering deep in thought. Did he have what it took to try out for a SEAL Team? There had been some professional football players and other athletes who'd made it, but many, like nearly 90% of them, hadn't. Did he have what it took?

The more he mulled it around in his mind, the more he strongly considered actually talking to a recruiter. Markham had told him he'd hook him up with someone who could help prepare him for a possible tryout. Unlike his Tottenham team, though, he'd have to enlist in the Navy, and if he didn't make a SEAL Team, he'd be making peanuts and serving his country on a ship or stationed somewhere in the world at a naval facility.

He wondered what Stephanie would say and then began to have second thoughts as he slipped his keycard into the motel room door and walked inside.

CHAPTER 8

STEPHANIE SLEPT IN, a luxury she rarely allowed herself. This was going to be her first day to herself, and she thought she'd go to the Farmer's Market, have a late breakfast and an espresso. It was going to be a hot day, and by eight o'clock, she'd closed up her bungalow and pulled the shades to keep it cool until nightfall. She was surprised she felt as good as she did and realized she hadn't awakened once last night. Her slumber had been long and deep.

She showered and put on a little makeup, grabbed a couple of plastic grocery bags, and headed downtown to the Market. It was a Wednesday, but since it was late summer time, there were lots of vendors with plenty of things she wanted to buy. She bought some fresh crab, sweet cherry tomatoes, some fresh basil, and lettuce. She grabbed some blue eggs from a local vendor who wasn't always there.

She brought her bounty home, rather than leave it

in the car, and then she walked downtown again for an omelet. On the way, she had an urge to call Patrick. He'd said he was staying over one more day and would be returning to his team tomorrow. He picked up his phone on the first ring.

"Hi there," she said.

"Ah, so that's who this is. Hi, Steph. How are you feeling this morning?"

"Much better. I've already been to the Farmer's Market, about to go have some brunch, and thought perhaps you'd like to join me."

"I'm just finishing up a meeting, but I can meet you someplace near downtown in like thirty minutes?"

She sat in the open-air café, watching the passersby while waiting for Patrick. He ambled past her table, not noticing her at first, but when he glanced around, she waved. With her emotions on more stable ground, she began to notice how handsome Patrick was. He had left stubble on his cheeks and chin, which accentuated his deep pink lips. He wore a light blue shirt with denim jeans and had spiked his hair with gel.

"What's so funny? Do I have something on my head?" he said, patting the top of his head.

"So funny seeing you with spikes."

"Oh, man, bad habit, I guess. The men overseas use more product on their hair than women do here. Hairspray…you name it."

"Well, they want to look good on camera."

He nodded and looked down at the little vase of flowers between them. "Yes, they do. Very vain."

And then there was that awkward silence. Looking at him full-on the way she had yesterday seemed today to feel too intimate. His taking her to the grammar school had felt deeply personal. And private. Though they didn't build on it, she felt it was the starting line, the platform, forged years ago when they were children. On that, they could agree. As to where their relationship was going…well, that would have to be to be another story.

They ordered their brunch, and while waiting, she decided to add some discussion to the awkwardness about their kiss yesterday and what it might portend.

"Ryan and I used to love coming here for late breakfast, when we could. Summer times are best for me since I don't have preschool. But he wasn't always home in the summer, so it was a treat when we could come here."

"This place used to be a bank or something when I left for Europe."

"Yes. It was."

"It's nice. I like it."

She was just thinking the same thing about his fresh-washed face and his smooth lips.

He looked to the side and watched an old man

cross the street. She could tell he had something he wanted to tell her, just like when they were kids. Then he poured the blue-eyed charm over her, gave her a crooked half-smile, and cocked his head. "I've made some decisions about my future."

She arched her eyebrows and leaned forward.

"I'm going to give the Teams a try, Steph."

Her heart dropped to the floor. His voice droned on, like she was listening to a conversation from under water.

He can't be serious.

"Why, Patrick?"

He carefully leaned back in his chair and watched her. "I want to do something like what Ryan did. Make a contribution. The pay is good with soccer, and I know it stinks in the Navy, but I've already figured that out. I'd have to make some huge adjustments, like sell my flat in London, and be careful with my spending habits. But I've saved quite a bit these past few years, and I could do it."

"I'm not talking about the money aspect. Why would you *willingly* put yourself in harm's way? You don't have to."

"Did Ryan have to? Really have to?"

She considered this. "Yes. I think he did. He was driven to be a warrior of some kind. He had this code of honor."

Patrick covered his mouth, leaned his head back, and looked at her beneath lowered eyelids, like he was looking through wire-rimmed bifocals. "And you don't think I have that code of honor?"

"No. That's not what I'm saying—"

"You don't think I put on the jersey of my team and play like a warrior? You don't see me like Ryan did, doing what Ryan did? Being a hero?"

The waiter brought their food, but now Stephanie wasn't hungry.

"Is that what you do, play the part of a hero?"

"It isn't a part, Steph. I *save* the ball. I *protect* the box. With my body."

"Seriously, Patrick, you don't think there is any comparison to—"

He suddenly leaned forward and placed his palm over hers. "Careful, Steph."

He refused to look at her for the rest of their meal. Stephanie knew she'd hit a nerve and regretted not holding back. She felt horrible.

He drove her to her house and parked the rental in front. They had ridden in silence. The distance between them suddenly felt wider than the ocean. Her heart was breaking from the pain of losing Ryan, and despite how guarded she'd been, she knew she had a new scar. Was the grieving process going to be like this? One of her friends had suggested she talk to someone, and she'd thought talking to Patrick would be the best choice, that together they could—*what?*

What had she expected? Neither of them was whole enough to really help the other. With the damage already done, she decided to level with him about a few things. Turning in her seat, she hoped he would understand what she was going to tell him.

"He had to do it, Patrick. He was *driven* to do it." She spoke to the side of his face. His profile would always be a thing of beauty. He was one of those men who could be considered pretty, he was so handsome. His nose was long and thin. His naturally tanned skin glowed in the sunlight, the dark stubble giving him just enough of the bad boy look to make him exciting and accentuate full, rosy lips. But despite his confident demeanor, she knew something was eating on him from the inside. She'd picked a scab. Would Patrick trust her with the knowledge of what it was? She continued.

"I didn't want Ryan to go onto the Teams. We didn't get married because I was so mad at him for just enlisting without telling me. We'd talked about it, and he'd completely misread how I felt. We should have talked more. But no, he just went and did it."

Patrick began to nod. "I remember that time." He inhaled and blew it all out. "I tried my darndest to talk him out of it, too. Of course, it was hard, because I was calling from London. I had no clout."

"Neither did I," she said.

"He wouldn't listen."

She saw moisture collect in the corner of his eye, then sighed and decided to keep talking anyway. "I was angry because I felt he'd put the Navy in front of me, and because he didn't consult me when he *knew* it was going to affect my whole life. We hadn't quite decided to get married at that point, but all the signs were pointing that way. We had a horrible fight that night. He accused me of secretly writing you, talking to you."

Patrick wrinkled his nose in disgust. "Me?"

"It's because we both told him the truth. We were both telling him the same things, in almost the same words."

"He didn't have anything to prove," Patrick murmured. She watched him struggle to hide the tears, even going so far as to tilt his head back against the headrest to hide them. "I must have said it a dozen times."

"And that's what I told him, too, Patrick. It probably sounded like we'd rehearsed it." She turned to face forward as she finished, "I told him I loved him just the way he was. He got really angry, so I finally told him if he joined the Teams, I wouldn't marry him. He went off to the Great Lakes Training Center without a girlfriend, Patrick. We broke it off. My heart was sick. I didn't hear from him for four months."

"I didn't know that. What changed your mind?"

"Ryan. I realized I was in love with him. I think I've always been in love with him. And the more I was around him, the more I became convinced I could do this." She felt her cheeks blush. "He was very charming. He won me over, tried really hard to be someone I could fall completely for, and he was right," she said to her lap. "And this, this—what happened to him—this is exactly what I was afraid of."

She was aware that Patrick sat motionless but was watching every strand of hair fall forward, every pucker and ripple of her blouse, every tear that coursed down her cheek. She tried not to notice the electric tension in the front seat or the way she started to feel his heat as he leaned forward, raised her chin with his thumb and forefinger, and said, in the sweetest apology she'd ever heard, "I'm sorry," before kissing her.

His kiss was even more intoxicating than the last one. He wasn't going to linger, so as he pulled away, she leaned into him and kept their mouths close. "It's not your fault," she whispered back while she studied those eyes the color of a summer sky.

She felt a tightening in her belly, and her clothes felt restrictive. It was heavenly to close her stinging eyes, which intensified the ache in her lower abdomen. Patrick kissed her eyelids, one by one, and then repeated it, as if applying some healing agent.

She didn't expect to hear his breath in her ear or to hear as his tongue wetted his lips, the nibbling sounds of little kisses under her ear, behind it, and then down her neck. She had never touched or even been this close to his forehead or inhaled his musky man scent and allowed it to wash over her.

She became putty in his hands, and the slow unwrapping of her soul when his fingers found her breasts and squeezed made her feel tethered to him. He was her shelter in the storm, the safe island in the middle of a raging emotional sea, and for right now, she'd take it, this one little taste of passion. The glow in her chest reminded her of the promise of another sunny day, regardless of the tragedy of the day before.

But just as every dream has a dawn, their moment together in the front seat couldn't go further for her. She suspected he could. Probably did. Probably did a lot.

It also bothered her that he planned to give up soccer and try out for the SEAL teams. Once again, she hadn't been part of that decision, not that she had a right to be in this case. But she didn't want to go there.

She'd been fairly proud of herself, but then the tears welled again, and this time it was her turn to lean back and stare at the visor. She took a deep breath, blew it out, and tried to settle the confusing things going on inside her body.

This is what it felt like to be fourteen. Even as a woman she could remember the passion boiling inside her back then and the total lack of experience and fear that overbalanced it. In the midst of that confusing tug of war, with the addition of a little time, she learned how to grow up and become a woman worthy of being loved.

When she didn't turn in his direction or even look at him, he removed his arm from behind her seat and placed both hands on the steering wheel. She didn't have to tell him tonight would not be that runaway train she used to dream about when she was little. She could still remember the lines she'd made up while she played with her dolls, "I love you. Let's get married. Let's have babies. Today."

"What's so funny?"

"I was just remembering what I thought a kiss was before I actually had one, except from my father or my little brother when I was forced to." She leaned back in the seat and smiled at Patrick—beautiful, strong, muscled Patrick, a man she could very easily stupidly fall in love with. "My parents lied."

"All right. So where does that leave us, Stephanie?"

"This could all go really fast, Patrick, and I guess I'm not sure yet if it's you I'm attracted to, or Ryan's replacement. That's not fair to either one of us."

"Fair enough. I'll walk you to your door."

"Thank you." But the driver side door was already closed by the time she'd answered him. He helped her up, which was always the most awkward for them ever since he'd learned how to tackle her and not hurt her. The coach had insisted the boys always had to help the "ladies" up afterward, but Ryan had told her Patrick always liked to take their hands and show them how strong he was.

It was no different today. She just hoped her heart could stand it long enough to begin healing on its own and not with the aid of someone she wanted to play equal partners with. Just like that feisty little girl with the messed-up face full of mud, she wanted to do it on her own first, get her bearings, and then, if there was anything left—well, time would have to take care of that.

They parted with no promises of future phone conversations, brunches, or talks, except Patrick did say, "You call me if you need anything. I'll be in the states for another ten days; then I'm pretty much hard to get hold of. But if you need to talk, Stephanie, I'm your guy."

She wished she could make him her guy in the real sense, but it just wasn't right, and it might never be.

With a chaste kiss on her cheek accompanied by her palm on his, they parted. She turned around briefly to capture the image of him getting back into his car.

Yes, Patrick, you are my guy.

CHAPTER 9

PATRICK HAD ALREADY met with Trevor Markham before he and Stephanie had brunch. Tonight, it was merely social, and he was looking forward to spending more time with men who had served with Ryan. They met at a local pub/brewery this time. He felt instantly at home with the large screen TVs showing soccer, plus the dart boards and Celtic folk music in the background. They hunched around one round table, their feet scuffing through the peanut shells and sawdust littering the floor.

He got some details of the few decisions he was going to have to make while they ordered beers.

"Don't go in there with a plan of action. Don't bring anything you'll mourn or get nervous about if it doesn't sustain you. Just keep your wits about you. Improvise, but make damned sure you pay fuckin' attention," Markham instructed.

"You go it alone or with a friend or two?" Patrick

asked him.

"This asshole," he pointed to an olive-skinned, muscled warrior with the most tightly clipped beard he had ever seen. "And this asshole," Markham gestured with his full palm to the man sitting directly across from him, who looked to be all of eighteen years of age and still sporting pimples.

"Make it easier?"

"You know our fuckin' motto? *Only easy day was yesterday?* Don't go lookin' for easy. That'll get you jacked up."

"Hey, I'm Jake, by the way. My little brother will be joining one of the next classes. You might be in the same one, if it all works out."

Patrick shook Jake's hand and pointed to his beard. "That thing's a work of art."

Jake flashed him a big, white, toothy smile, which made the heavy gold chain he wore flash in the high intensity lights nearby. "I indulge when we're not deployed, but over there," he wiggled his eyebrows and let his eyes go crazy, "I don't cut anything."

"This fuckin' guy likes Brazilian waxing."

Patrick rolled his shoulder. "Nothin' wrong with that. The Europeans are into that shit too. Real common. The ladies, too," Patrick said casually.

"See, Trev. I'm a trendsetter," Jake said to his LPO.

"Yeah, but think how much more sleep you'd get

each day if you didn't spend all that time manicuring your hedge. Jake, you gotta find a lady who can take care of that for you."

Jake's grin was infectious. Patrick liked him immediately and made a mental note to find out how to contact him to get the number for his brother. "Jake, where you from?" he asked.

"I'm just a Heinz mixture, man. Brazilian—"

A sandy-haired, tanned kid sitting on the other side of Trevor interrupted. "See, that's where he gets that crazy notion he gotta be hairless. Fuckin' Brazilians, man."

Jake rolled with it, and Patrick soon realized there wasn't much he got upset about. He found it refreshing. "Anyway, Patrick, I've never met any of my relatives, except my little brother, Tyson. We grew up in foster care and each foster mother made up another story. We picked up a little bit from here, a little bit from there and—voila—you got your basic bad-ass family heritage. No pictures and shit. I got a granddad who was a Sioux chief, a grandma who cooked for rich folks in NOLA. I love Italian food, so there must be some of that in there, too."

Several men chuckled and took long draws on their beers.

"I don't even know if Tyson is my real brother, but they always tried to keep us together when one of us messed up and we had to change families. So, there must be something on file, not that it matters much. He's my brother fair and square."

Patrick knew it was tougher on Jake than he let on. "So, the Navy made you a man," he said.

"Hell no. The SEAL training made me a man. No excuses and stuff. I finally got it all dialed in that doing things right would keep me out of trouble, keep me alive, and damn, it's way more fun having a brotherhood behind you, right?"

"Here you go. I'll second that," Markham said as he raised his glass and they all toasted.

"Can I ask you a question?" Patrick asked the group.

"Sure," Trevor answered.

"What about girls? Any of you guys married?"

They all shook their heads. "Those guys don't go on these types of trips, on account it's a little tough on the wives to see this shit, know what I mean? I mean if they knew him, or knew the wife, well, that's a different story. Then everyone comes. But we don't like to separate the guys from their ladies when we get home. Bad for morale." Trevor Markham was not smiling.

Patrick nodded. "I'm guessing the wives stick together too."

"Oh yeah!" Jake said, nodding with emphasis. "She's gotta fit in like a little piece of the puzzle. If she doesn't, they aren't gonna make it."

Patrick frowned.

"We got a high divorce rate. She's got to like it as much as he does, or it never works." That comment echoed around in his brain, and he realized Stephanie, although beautiful and just his type, would in all likelihood be a casualty of his decision. He didn't like that thought, but he had time to sort it out, and until he signed that paper, anything could happen. The fact that she needed time didn't bode well for the two of them, and that was a shame. But it would be the best for her. He resigned himself to that, at least.

"So, they flew the lot of you?" Patrick looked from face to face until he returned to Trevor, "You all came up together?"

"Hell, no. I'm the only one here who was actually in the arena with Ryan. These guys were medical for this rotation. And Spencer here is a virgin, just came along for the action. But we all knew Ryan. I'm the one who brought him home."

The catcalls began in earnest, while Spencer squirmed and turned bright red.

"I'll have you know that's just for deployment." Spencer looked like Clark Kent without the glasses.

"We call him the professor," Trevor chortled.

As their food arrived, Patrick was also warned to be realistic, that with a ten percent pass rate, odds weren't in his favor. He knew the only thing he had going for him was that he'd kept that promise to himself since childhood, the promise not to fail at any team he tried out for. Quitting wasn't an option. They'd have to bury him or carry him away before that would happen. He didn't have to be the best at anything; he just would outlast everyone.

"That's good," Jake said, making Patrick realize he'd said it out loud. "You can use that. I like it."

Tomorrow, he'd sort out what he would tell his manager when he returned to the team. He was worried about what he would tell Ronnie, his best friend and soon-to-be-ex-defender on the squad. But he was most concerned that this decision might ultimately drive a stake through any chance of a relationship with Stephanie. In a sick kind of way, he was grateful she'd stopped his forward advance before they'd jumped into bed and it got complicated.

What are you saying? It's already complicated.

Maybe he would be allowed one more trip back to California before they started their season in Europe. She could meet him in San Diego. They could take it slow, much slower, so she wouldn't bolt again. He owed her that respect. And if she didn't want to see him…well, he'd have to accept that and move on. It would be good, though, to get it established one way or the other, so he could concentrate on his plans.

Nothing he found out about the SEALs gave him any pause. They looked him straight in the eyes. They had egos, but not attitudes. They joked, but they didn't belittle or bully anyone. They had to be light-hearted but ready for anything. He suspected they all knew exactly how many people were in the bar and how many of them carried weapons. He saw Trevor size up several large men Patrick had already decided he didn't care for. But what he liked best was that they weren't vying for attention or making a spectacle of themselves. They looked like they wanted to be respected, and then ignored.

He always thought you could tell a lot about a man by watching how he drank with his friends. Since his coaches on the professional level didn't go into long speeches like American football players were used to getting, the local watering hole was where the team bonding happened. He suspected it was the same with the SEALs.

He became more and more comfortable with his decision.

NEXT AFTERNOON, HIS plane landed in Ohio, and he raced to catch up with the team at their designated hotel. He was running late, and the squad was already assembled in the lobby waiting for the busses to take them to practice. Ronnie, as always, was to be his roommate.

"Do I have time to run up and change quick?" he asked his coach. The man scowled and nodded, first at Ronnie and then toward the elevators. Ronnie ran alongside him, clutching his personal equipment bag. He punched the key to the third floor.

"You okay, mate?" Ronnie asked.

"It was tough, Ronnie." They rode the elevator and then burst out and down the hallway. He followed Ronnie to their room. The defender inserted his key. "It was a beautiful ceremony," Patrick said while he dumped his bag on one of the beds and yanked out his keeper jersey and backup glove bag. "Met some of Ryan's SEAL buddies," he said while he pulled the bright green shirt over his head.

"Supposed to be fine lads, them SEALs."

He wanted to be careful not to let his intentions leak out until he had a plan in place. "Enjoyed talking to them about what they do. Ryan was one of their favorites, and he sacrificed himself to save a handful of Marines and two SEALs."

"That's messed up, Paddy."

Patrick busied himself tying his shoes, finding his cleats and second backup gloves, stuffing them into his team bag. "No. It's what Ryan wanted." He hadn't slept well last night and wondered how his lack of sleep would affect his performance in the box today at practice. When he looked up, Ronnie was staring at him with his hands on his hips.

"Fuck sake, Paddy. You're not thinkin' of following ol' Ryan into the ground now, are you?"

He hated to lie to Ronnie, especially since Ronnie himself wouldn't be on the squad after this year. "I admit it's tempting, Ronnie. I had a good long discussion with them. A man could do worse."

They headed out the door, running for the elevator.

"Shit, Patrick, you'd make, what, one tenth the salary? For what? Gettin' yourself blown up? Riddled with holes, man?"

The doors closed. A young couple was standing in the corner, dwarfed by the large defender and the giant next to them.

"Hi, folks," Patrick waved to them. They huddled closer to each other and said nothing.

Ronnie had spoken the truth. But for Patrick, it wasn't about the money. It was the adventure and the honor of it.

In his own way, he looked at serving on the Teams as the *real* beautiful game.

"You Yanks do the dumbest things for being such smart blokes," Ronnie said.

"Yeah? Well, we beat you guys, didn't we?"

CHAPTER 10

STEPHANIE MISSED A call from Patrick when she was working out. In his voice message he said he'd arranged to come to San Diego for a couple of days, maybe a week, and wanted to know if she could meet him there.

Call me after 5 today, she'd texted back.

He'd not said why he would be coming to San Diego. She had a niggling fear that this had something to do with his decision to enlist.

"Stephanie, first I want to say something, okay?" She heard when her phone rang at exactly five, and he began talking before she could get it to her ear. Her heart pounded. She had been watching the phone as it counted down the last twenty minutes. The electric thrill that he'd called right on the dot at five o'clock meant something.

"I've been thinking, now that we're practicing harder. Funny how that straightens out things. Draw a little blood, and I stop feeling sorry for myself." His voice was gravelly. She remembered how she tingled hearing it. She was tingling now.

"I want to apologize."

She went into high alert.

"Yesterday morning was very hard for me."

So far so good, but when he hesitated, she couldn't help but blurt out, "Patrick, just tell me. I'm not a fragile doll, here. I can tell you have something you want to say, and you don't want to say it. Well, quit making me wait for it."

"Come visit me in San Diego, Steph. Give me a chance to—"

"Charm me?" She instantly wished she'd not responded and could eat her words.

Patrick laughed. "Well, there is that. Maybe. What do you think?"

"About what?"

"About visiting me in San Diego."

"What am I supposed to think, Patrick?" She decided to soften her tone. "I guess it depends on what you have in mind?"

"I want to talk. I want to spend time with you. I want you to come to San Diego because you want to, not to do me or anyone else a favor."

She was telling him yes before she could stop herself.

"Are you sure you're ready? You're Ryan's girl."

It struck her as funny in a quirky way. "Where did you plan on taking me, to a dungeon or something? I didn't say I was going to have sex with you. I'm coming for a visit. And for the record, does this have anything to do with the Navy?"

"Yes. I want to talk to you that and a few other things, if you'll listen."

"When?" she finally asked.

"I'm thinking Friday. Can you spend the week? You could fly home next Sunday?"

"You were thinking, or you bought your tickets?"

"What? Look, Stephanie, do you want to come to San Diego or not? It's a simple question."

He was right. Time to decide. "Sure."

"Good. Friday night, I get in about six. You wanna catch a flight that gets in about the same time, if you can, or, better yet, I'll get the tickets."

"No, I'll do it."

"Actually, I'm going to insist. Sorry if that pisses you off. We have a lot to discuss. It's important to me. And I can easily afford it."

No, that didn't piss her off at all. "Well, in that case. Sure."

"I'll work on it and text you the results."

"Sounds good." She waited for him to reply.

"Coming home again, seeing you, seeing Ryan's

friends, it's had a big impact on me. Now I'm just trying to sort all that out. I'm looking forward to spending time with you again, Stephanie. I mean it."

"Me too, Patrick. But please, no pressure. We'll just see what happens," she followed her comment with a nervous giggle.

"Fair enough, Steph. Look, I gotta go."

"Until Friday, then." She hung up, so she didn't have to feel any more of that awkward tension that had started up again.

Friday took forever to come. She'd been so preoccupied she'd nearly wrecked her car once. When one of her fellow teachers offered to take her to the airport, she accepted gratefully. She had little to say on the way there. For some reason, her friend gave her a big hug, like her mother had done when she went off to college. She would come back changed. How was still a mystery. But it was thrilling.

The flight would be short, but the wait was long. She watched couples kiss, single servicemen in and out of uniform sitting in groups with their duffle bags. Young recruits spoke wide-eyed with older, more seasoned veterans with chiseled abs, covered in tattoos. She got respectful nods from most of the men ready to board the plane. She was surprised how quiet the group was, especially for a Friday night on the way to a vacation paradise like San Diego.

With the flight completely full, she sat next to a couple of young, muscled men she identified as some Special Forces guys. They struck up a conversation with her and somehow it leaked out about Ryan. Their compassion and condolences didn't help her nerves. She begged out of the conversation, even though she knew they were probably SEALs. She still needed time with her private thoughts.

When the plane touched down, she was startled, having fallen asleep. She texted Patrick, and he promised to meet her by baggage claim. Quickly, she gathered her things and made her way down the aisle to the terminal. She had no checked luggage, but Patrick was there with a warm smile, looking way more handsome and refined than he had a right to. In his left hand, he held a dozen red roses.

While not the expected greeting, it was exactly what her heart had dared to hope for.

HE'D BEEN NERVOUS about seeing her. The flowers were more for his benefit than hers, trying to make a bold statement to give himself courage. He knew they had to have *that talk*. He wanted to explain things to her and do it right. He hoped to God, and even asked Ryan for his help, so he would get it right.

"Hey, beautiful," he said while she approached him with her fresh looks. Her round brown eyes sparkled, her lashes demurely downcast. He enjoyed that she was embarrassed. She wasn't like any of the women he'd told himself he needed. His anonymous sexual partners were strung together like tangled netting in the box, all knotted up sometimes, running into each other. Stephanie was the model by which he had judged all other women. It had been that way for years, but he'd just figured it out. And now she was standing in front of him.

She looked down at the roses, sniffed them, and smiled. "Nice." He could see she was anxious. She kept looking at the flowers, and then his feet, and his fingers holding the flowers, but she wasn't looking into his eyes.

"Come here, Stephanie," he whispered.

She quickly darted a look to his face, and that's when he was overcome. He grabbed her, pulling her close to him, and holding her to his body, then kissed her hard. He didn't want anything misunderstood. The flowers said one thing. His kiss was going to tell her something else.

At first, she was stiff, but then she eased into it, and, at last, melted. He felt her heart racing, loved the muffled moans she gave him while he plunged deep inside her mouth. Cradling her head under his chin, he hugged her. "I've been an idiot, Stephanie."

She nodded slightly in agreement, which sent his

heart soaring. She pulled away and drilled him with a look. "I think we both have."

"Fair enough." He extended the roses to her, taking her carryon and slipping his arm around her waist as they made their way through crowds of passengers. He watched as she buried her nose in the bouquet. It would have felt even better if she'd leaned into him. But he was going to work on his patience.

"Hope you're hungry," he said.

"Actually, starved. I didn't eat all day."

"That apprehensive?" He looked down at her, but she didn't return his gaze.

Her lack of response was bothering him.

They drove to the marina near the convention center. Helping her out of the car, he took her hand to lead her to the restaurant that had been recommended. "I'm just getting my bearings. Visited Ryan down here once, but I wasn't in any condition to remember a thing."

She said nothing, but stared straight ahead with an unreadable expression. So, he kept talking.

"Ryan had just made it through BUD/S and, man, was he sore. He was bleeding in places I didn't know men bled. His feet were green from wearing those boots and socks for five days straight. We got a room down right there," he pointed to the multistoried hotel overlooking the marina, "and I had to practically force him to take a shower. He was falling asleep while he took his clothes off. I thought he'd fall asleep in the shower and drown."

"I remember him telling me about that. His parents were so proud he'd made it through."

"I think they'd cut about two thirds of the class by that time. You wouldn't have wanted to see him. He was a mess."

"Surprised he wanted to party."

"Not that night. We put a movie on the TV, and I don't think he stayed awake long enough to get through the opening credits. I let him sleep. We partied long and hard the next day and night, though."

The restaurant was right where he'd been told, overlooking the twinkling water and boats at the marina. Ushered to their table, he asked if she wanted wine, and she declined. She declined a beer, too, but he ordered one.

"Ryan—"

She stopped him by covering his hand on the table. "Patrick, why are we talking about Ryan?"

He'd rehearsed what he wanted to say so many times he'd forgotten his lines. Over-preparation, like on the field. Mentally preparing for one style of play and having the opposing team go at it a completely different way. Games were lost when the opponent got inside your head. Stephanie was getting inside his head big time.

"I'm sorry."

"You sure do spend a lot of time telling me you're sorry. I'm getting double messages here, Patrick."

He was totally confused. This is the part of being with a woman that frustrated him, had been the sole reason he'd never hooked up with anyone for more than a couple of dates. Women were so confusing, so difficult to read. When he was defending the box, he could tell which foot the forward was going to use every time, but he didn't have a clue what was going on with Stephanie. He began to think having her come down to San Diego had been a colossal mistake.

"Try just telling me the truth, Patrick." Her sweet voice washed over him, and it steadied his nerves.

"I'm leaving soccer to try out for the SEAL teams, Stephanie. I've done some research on what it would take, no guarantees. But I want to give it a try."

"What? You had me fly down here to tell me this?"

"Not entirely."

"There's more?"

"Yes. I wanted to explain my decision."

"Okay. We could have done this by phone."

No way, ma'am. He had a goal to achieve tonight. It had nothing to do with scoring, either. It had everything to do with laying a firm foundation for something bigger than that.

"Wanted to tell you in person."

"Okay."

"I love playing soccer. I love the money. I love my teammates. And yes, I enjoyed the girls." He searched her eyes but didn't find judgment there. "Steph, there have been lots of girls. I need you to know that."

"Okay. What makes you think you're the only one?"

He hesitated for a second before he saw her smile. "Don't look at me that way, Patrick. Ryan was only my second."

He blushed in spite of himself. He still didn't feel at ease with her, although she was encouraging him. Or at least she wasn't rejecting him.

"I wanted to make sure you were okay with my decision."

She leaned back in her chair, arms crossed. "So where is this going?"

"None of that past matters to me. Point is, coming home has changed me. I didn't expect I would ever want to give up soccer, and now I do. I can see it. I want to do something else with my life. Make a difference somehow."

"Okay. You want my blessing, is that it?" She kept her arms crossed.

"Yes. It's important to me."

She leaned forward, placing her chin on her folded fingers, her elbows on the table. "Tell me why, Patrick."

Her eyes didn't flinch.

This was the *do-or-die* moment for him. He hoped he'd given it enough explanation that she'd feel comfortable with what he'd been rehearsing all afternoon.

"I want to see if we can work something out together, Steph. What I'm saying is that I want to try. We'll take it slow, but that's what I want, and I want to be honest with you about all of this. You also need to understand I want to become a SEAL, too. If I don't make a team, I'll be in the Navy. There's no buyout of a contract clause in the enlistment. There's no guarantee I won't become a cook on a carrier, although I can't cook, so that's probably a long shot. I could be a—"

"Patrick, would you look at me?"

That's when he realized he'd been looking everywhere else but at her. He couldn't tell if she was angry or just confused. "Look, Stephanie, we know each other. I mean we know more about each other than most married couples, I think. I know we haven't spent much time around each other for several years, but once you know someone that well, I think you always know them. We'd be perfect together. We have the—"

"Patrick, shut up."

He didn't notice she'd interrupted him. Her steady brown eyes gazed back at him, and she was smiling. Finally, she was smiling. He angled his head to make sure he'd heard her right.

"I'll give it a try," she whispered, taking his hand.

"Tomorrow, I go over and check things out. I wanted you there, too. Next, I have to go back formally buy out my contract."

"Will that be a problem?"

"They've always got talent stacked up, so they've got two perfectly good keepers they've been grooming. I think the club will actually benefit financially if I leave." He watched their fingers entwine on the tabletop. "I wanted to be sure you were okay with my decision. I thought you could get your questions answered, and there are some people you could talk to—"

"Do you think Ryan and I ever talked about this?"

"Right." Of course, they had. What was he thinking?

"So what's your schedule like, do you have any idea?"

"It'll take a few weeks to get processed and released from the Tottenham team. I sign up at the Recruitment Center, and it all depends on when they have a spot. They might want me to ship out the next day, which I cannot do until I'm released. More than likely, it's hurry up and wait. Not like the published schedules they do for Tottenham."

"So when would you move out here?" she asked as her eyes showed that coyness he loved, snagging his heart.

"How about tomorrow? We could find a place to rent. I could try to get out here a few days here and there."

She giggled at that. "Never in a million years did it occur to me that this morning I'd be thinking about moving here." Then she frowned.

"I'd like to start looking for a place right away, if that's agreeable."

"You worried I'll change my mind?"

"I don't want to let you get away."

"I've always been here, Patrick. I think that's why this keeps moving so fast. I promised myself I wouldn't do that, but here I am."

"Yes. Here you are. It feels right, Stephanie. You could come back with me to England. We get the release and travel a bit around Europe, have a little time to ourselves. And then we get serious with the Navy."

"I'd have to help them find a replacement for the upcoming school year, but then I could go. That actually sounds like fun."

"Okay. You join me in, what, a couple of weeks?"

"Here or in London?"

"Why not? You ever see London during the holidays? It's outstanding." He pulled her fingers to his lips.

Holy shit. She actually said yes.

THE WAITER CAME to take their order. They gazed at each other. The standoff soon got smoldering, while her beautiful eyes softened and the crease at the right side of her mouth dimpled as her lips curled up into a sultry smile that could only mean one thing.

Without taking his eyes off of her, he said, "I think we're going to have dessert first." She tilted her head and saluted him with her water glass. Finally, they were on the same page. The waiter mumbled something about going to get the dessert menu, and she stopped him.

"I'm sorry, but we're going to have dessert somewhere else. But thanks." She didn't look at the waiter, either, even though the young man tried to get their attention.

Their attention was riveted elsewhere.

CHAPTER 11

PATRICK HAD BOOKED a room overlooking the water at a nearby hotel. Their view of the moonlight on the harbor was like a movie set. Without turning on the lights, they dropped their bags and walked to the window. His arms went around her waist. Stephanie felt comfortable, settled, even though things were moving at lightning speed, like surf swallowing up a huge hole left in the sand. Her vacant insides needed to be filled with life and hope for a beautiful tomorrow.

She wondered what Ryan would think and concluded he would approve. If he couldn't be there, he would choose Patrick—not to take his place, but to care for Stephanie—because he knew he could always count on his best friend, and because he also knew she had always carried a torch for him.

It would be difficult being alone again after Patrick left for England, but it was an important opportunity to start putting the past to rest. She didn't want to erase those wonderful memories of Ryan, memories she'd always have. But it would be painful to remain in the town where she and Ryan had fallen in love, to see all the places they used to go, meet people they'd talked to as a couple. It seemed healthy for her to start fresh in another location, in a country she'd never been to, with someone she had always loved and trusted showing her the way.

"Your thoughts?" he whispered in her ear.

"Just was wondering what it would be like to visit England. Never been anywhere outside the country."

"You'll love it. Can't wait to show you." He began kissing her neck.

"Everything's gone so fast."

"Yes. It has." He held her chin up leading her lips to his. "And it's been twenty some years in the making too. That doesn't seem so fast, does it?"

She gulped in air at the thrilling possibilities for an evening of lovemaking, of having Patrick's hands on her body for the first time.

"Hey, you okay with everything? Truth. Tell me the truth."

"I'm fine tonight and will be fine tomorrow. When you go back to England, that's when I'll fall apart."

"But not tonight. Are you sure about being okay with my decision?"

She liked that he didn't want to take advantage. "As

long as you're okay with it. What if you don't make the Teams?"

"Most people don't. But I have an inside track, Steph."

"Really? What is it?"

"Ryan. He told me the secret."

"You're kidding. Tell me."

"I think he meant more than just trying out for the Teams. He meant it about life in general. He said the secret was never to quit. At anything."

That was like him, she thought. That's why her going on with her life was the right thing to do, even though perhaps there would be a bumpy road ahead.

He waited for her to kiss him, though she could feel the lodge pole in his pants. She loved that he wanted to be careful with her, even though there was no doubt as to the evening's trajectory.

After their kiss, and without saying a word, he led her solemnly to the bed.

His hands were deliberate and sure. Slowly, he unpeeled her clothing, kissing her down the back of her spine, sliding his long fingers down her belly to the juncture between her legs. She held his hand and moved her sex onto his palm, giving herself to him. The hitch in his breath told her everything she needed to know. He'd never been shy around women, so this was so special.

With gentle motions, he touched her with respect. His hand guided their relationship further, down a path that would forever alter and obliterate the space between them.

She could hear the sounds of foghorns in the distance and a bell somewhere farther down the beach. Was that someone quitting a BUD/S class? She knew she wouldn't quit. Patrick's long, powerful thighs urged her toward the bed, and she heard the bell again.

He turned her, pulling her back into his chest and gently squeezing her breast with their joined hands. With the other, he moved aside her long hair and kissed her neck. Their bodies swayed to a silent lover's rhythm. His upper torso completely and warmly protected her back.

HE WAS ACHING for her, but aching more to know if she could feel the magic he felt.

His fingers slipped up her neck and into her hair as he pressed his forehead against her scalp. He allowed her to hear his heavy breathing, allowed her to feel his erection now reaching the waistband of his slacks. She permitted his left hand to smooth their way down her firm abdomen, giving him full access to breach the top of her skirt. She separated her legs and arched back into him so deliciously. His fingers easily found the wetness in her juncture. She was willing and open to him in ways he'd never felt before. He knew her desire for him was rising by the second, matching his own.

"God, Stephanie. I—"

She'd whispered soothing words to him that tingled and reverberated inside his head like tiny diamond crystals. She melted further into his arms.

His kiss and need to see her expression were crucial. He read her as he closed his mouth over hers, as they lazily played with each other's tongues. He inhaled at the warm feeling of her fingers exploring his abdomen, sliding up and under his shirt, her palms to his naked skin, her arms now wrapped around his neck, her knees spread to the sides so she could rub herself against his thigh, ride his thigh when he raised it, lifting her and allowing her legs to nearly dangle so the full weight of her body could ride him there.

Open your eyes, Stephanie. Look at me. I am real. I am alive and in your arms. Is this what you want? He needed to know it was his body she loved, his body she craved, his mouth she wanted to feel tasting her. When he lifted her chin to him again and brushed her cheeks with his thumbs she did open her eyes.

"Oh, Patrick. I've always loved you. Help me to heal."

Of course he could be that guy. Of course he wanted to help her. If afterwards the unthinkable happened and they couldn't make things work, he'd have to be okay with that, because right now, it was about Stephanie. And he knew he was the only man who would be able to take away at least part of her pain. Not all of it, but enough for now.

"Are you sure that is okay with you? Just want to be sure you are—"

"I need to feel you inside me, Patrick."

"Oh, baby, thank God," he whispered to her lips.

She giggled, like she felt shy. He became shy as well. He thought about the school grounds where he first fell in love with her as a child and where he'd understood recently he could love her now as a man. That she could be his woman. It had taken him over twenty years, and here he was, right back there, standing on the playground of long ago, waiting for her to show up in all her pinkness.

How he'd played that image on repeat in his mind over the years. But this time, this night, he would be making her his. It was a dream he'd had for as long as he could remember. He didn't have to share her with the entire school or the twenty years of her life it took to bring her back to him. Their past was their past. She was about to give him her present.

SHE CLIMBED UNDER the sheets, and Patrick pulled them off her.

"I want to see you, Stephanie. All of you."

She could barely make out his face in the moonlight when he slowly kissed his way down her belly, fingering her sex, causing her back to arch in pleasure. His thumb pressed down on her nub, making her cry out in need of him. Patrick was as tender as she expected he would be, yet even more so. His sensual lips kissed her deeply while their tongues played, sending her into waves of need. She wanted to tell him the only thing that came to mind as he worked his way in and out, as his kisses commanded obedience:

More.

Was it possible to need more than to enjoy the sex? Did this need encompass everything about their relationship?

Whatever it was, she would ride this tide of pleasure, and if she was lucky, he'd stay right with her. He'd catch fire like she was. She wanted to ignite whatever fantasies he may have had at one time in his life, become that woman he desired more than all others. She would not rest until his surrender to her was equal to hers to him.

When at last he mounted her, she heard a distant sea bird crying like it was the last of her tragic tears. She'd not be alone any longer. She heard the water lapping under the pier, and the metal clanging on the masts of the boats moored there. His breathing was ragged, sounding like waves crashing on shore.

This was right, and this was true.

She'd learned how fragile life was and how it could be snuffed out unexpectedly. She was in it for the long haul. She'd face everything she needed to face in the coming weeks and months. She'd do it honestly, and she'd let her love handle the fear of what was to come.

She'd hold this man in her heart, like she held him now. And she vowed she'd never quit.

CHAPTER 12

PATRICK HAD ALWAYS given Ryan a hard time about the sun in San Diego. It was hell on a hangover. But one thing he could not deny was that it was wonderful for lingering in bed for some early morning, then mid-morning, and followed by late morning sex.

He was sure there wouldn't be a fourth round, but damn if she didn't just turn on everything inside him like it was Christmas, Fourth of July, and Opening Day at the stadium playing in front of the Royal Family.

By the way she lazily lay back with her arm over her head, her honey-brown hair invitingly splayed all over the white pillow, that half smirk and special twinkle in those sleep-deprived brown eyes of hers, she knew she'd surprised him. It wouldn't be good form to comment on that. Their love was too fragile and early. But holy hell, the sex was strictly old school and full-out passionate, unlike anything he'd ever experienced. Nice thing about it was it felt clean, right, and wasn't enhanced by alcohol.

Well, that's because she's mine now.

Yes, her heart was still snagged on Ryan, and it always would be, and that would be okay with Patrick. But now, this little lady, quickly becoming his reason for living, belonged to him. She'd not like to hear it that way, but a man knew what that felt like without any apology. He was mated just as solidly as those dark vampires she liked to read in her romance novels. It was a feeding from one soul to another, and back again.

Last night had been a burst of the senses that washed away the bad memories of all the past hookups and back seat quickies. Now he wanted to do all those things with Stephanie. He wanted to see her naked anywhere and everywhere. He wanted to see her as a good girl with her pink lunchbox containing a pink vibrator he could use all over her, see her in a uniform without panties, in a soccer jersey—in *his* soccer jersey—so he could smell her pheromones all during a game. He'd stretch and extend more. He'd catch every fucking ball that came within a half a field of him. He felt great, like he could go for ten games straight without any rest. He'd rip the legs off anyone who came at him with their cleats up. It would be career ending for the unfortunate baller, he felt so strong.

"Penny for your thoughts?" she asked in a sultry

whisper, closing her eyes halfway for emphasis.

He licked his lips. What would he taste next, now that he had his breath back? Veeger was beginning to get hard again, and that little anatomical part was demanding all the blood in his body, so he couldn't think to give her a proper answer.

So he just smiled.

"There! That look," she exclaimed, reaching under the sheets and then letting her eyes go all wide, faking surprise at his hardness. She hand-stroked him, and then she squeezed his balls.

After he sucked in all the air in the room, he whispered, "Miss Stephanie, I had no idea a preschool teacher could fuck so fantastic. I was prepared for the sermon, but you had the choir, the big pipe organ, and the tympany going too."

She liked hearing that and giggled, showing off that soft velvet beneath her chin and the jiggling flesh at the top of her chest. Just the way she writhed in bed when she laughed turned him on. He was going to be a mess tomorrow, but he didn't care.

He drew up to her ear and whispered, "Man, I'm wiped and ready to go again. You're going to send me back emaciated, a mere shadow of myself."

"That's because I don't want you to forget me when you get back to the team."

"Not a possibility, honey. But I have to ask you

something."

She pushed him at the shoulders and examined his face at arm's length, worried. "Ask me what?"

He tried to keep a straight face, but failed, burying his head in her chest instead, laughing.

"What?" she insisted again. She clutched at his scalp, attempting to raise his head by pulling his hair.

"You said Ryan was only your second?" He was going to burst a gut, but he held his laughter in.

She nodded.

"What the hell was the *first* guy thinking? How in the dickens was he so stupid to let you go?"

Her smile was cautious. "I wasn't very smart. Happened by accident the night Ryan left for Great Lakes. I thought we were done. I was heartbroken."

This was concerning. "So is that what this is?" He knew it was a big mistake the instant he said it and winced. "Sorry."

Her warm hands flew up to his face, and she nearly pulled the ears right off him. "Don't you ever say that again, Patrick. This is *real*. This is no recovery from a nightmare. This is what I was made for."

"Honey, I'm sorry." He placed his palm gently against her forehead and brushed it with his thumb. "And about the being made for this," he continued by kissing her down her neck then crossed over to her midsection and sucked at her belly button, "that's affirmative. Except you were made for *me*, honey. And I like how all the pieces fit and how wonderful all this feels."

THEY CHECKED INTO a rental agency and got a list of houses and apartments available for rent. Patrick felt himself blush because their open affection made them the center of so much attention everywhere they went. They drove through various neighborhoods until he focused on a duplex midway between the strand and the beach on Coronado Island. Stephanie was game to try to rent it.

"This is as expensive as Palo Alto. I can't afford to live here," she said, after reviewing the list of rental units on the island from the agency.

"Not your concern. You're a kept woman, Steph. I pick up this tab—depending on how much I have to give the team to buy out my contract."

"What if they don't let you out?"

"Then I go postal on them."

She hit him with the sheaf of papers. "No, really, Patrick. What if I get situated down here and then you can't leave Tottenham?"

"They have to. It's in my contract. There's even a suggested value they need to be within ten percent of. Not like I'm Rinaldo or Pele. And it frees up some cash. My contract was going to be up in two years anyway." Then he added, "And we have a couple of guys who live in Germany and a couple Africans who fly home whenever they can. Leave their families there and sort of commute."

"That's just nuts."

"You have to understand many guys from other countries don't have the connections and can't get their families visas anyway. And it's cheaper in their native country besides." He also knew that running around chasing women was a big pastime with the teams and suspected that factored into those decisions.

"So they won't really care?"

"I wouldn't say that. If they scream too loud, they might get more money out of me, but it's something that's done all the time. Just like if another team was interested in me, I have a covered clause where I can go, if the other team pays enough. Not like it is in the States. Oh, and they can retain me for several games in the new season, but I'm going to try to get out of that. Otherwise, we might spend a little time in London. You'd like that, wouldn't you?"

"I would. What about the apartment?"

"We keep it."

"And the Navy?"

"I wait on them. They tell me when the class starts. I go to Great Lakes, just like Ryan did. Then the four phases. The pay will suck, but I've saved. I'll not even earn what my bonus would have been."

"I know you'll make it."

He felt the same way but didn't want to jinx it by saying so. "You just keep praying for me. Knowing I'll get to come home to you. That might just give me that extra bit of motivation to get me over the top. You know what Ryan went through."

She got that far away look again and nodded absent-mindedly.

They drove his rental car to the beach and watched the waves. They held hands and didn't say a word. It was so damned fast, all this. But just like their first night together, it felt clean—an honest beginning.

"So should we do this?" he asked.

Her warm brown eyes spoke of her innocence and complete trust in him. "I think if I don't do it, Patrick, I'll regret it the rest of my life."

He completely agreed.

Before they left the island, Patrick gave the rental company a fat check to hold the apartment, with the rent starting the first of the next month. That would give Stephanie three weeks to give her notice and begin the move-in. Patrick was going to detach from the Spurs as soon as the friendly season was over and head back to California to help with the move.

Two days later, Patrick went with Chief Petty Officer Trevor Markham to visit Lt. Eugene Forestall, the recruiter Markham had told him about.

"First of all, you don't believe his bullshit," Markham started.

"I thought you were friends."

"Oh, we are, but I never take their lies for granted. They lie as much as they drink, and recruiters always drink a bunch. He has no idea what it takes to become a SEAL, so he's going to tell you there are things that will be better for your future."

"Like what?"

"Dental school. Submarines."

"I have no interest in either of those fields."

"They're gonna act like they own you, but don't fall for it. It will be all smiles and handshakes and assurances. You make them put it in writing before you sign up today, if that's what you're here to do."

"That's my intention."

Just as Markham had described, Lt. Forestall was used to glad-handing everyone who walked into the door like he'd been pressing his uniform and filing his nails and waiting for him for two hours. Like he was Forestall's best friend.

He was a big man, about six foot seven, slightly taller than Patrick, but with a lot more meat on him. He had a wide gap between his two front teeth that gave him a pronounced lisp when he talked. On a big man, the lisp was distracting and hard to listen to without laughing.

"I'm sure your drinking buddy here has told you about the SEALs, but we got all kinds of programs here in the Navy that are even better." He leaned across the desk. "The SEALs are just for show, you know that, right? The Navy likes to parade them around foreign countries to make them think the whole military is like them. Actors. Fucking actors."

Markham growled, and Lt. Forestall went into a fit of belly laughter. Patrick didn't find it funny at all, but then the recruiter didn't know he'd just lost his best friend, Ryan. Patrick decided he didn't like the guy and certainly didn't trust him.

He tolerated the lecture and demonstration of the different programs outlined in glossy brochures. There was a movie running at the side of his office, projecting on the wall, showing pictures of pontoon boats spraying greenish water along a swampy riverbank. One of the occupants in the boat shot a large tuna-shaped fish leaping from the water, trying to escape the noisy craft. The screen displayed the words, *They Appreciate Wildlife.*

Forestall noticed his preoccupation with the movie. "Those are the SWCC boat guys. They do the extractions, mostly SEALs or joint Special Force commands, and equipment. Lots of action and very dangerous. You seem like a way smarter fella than that."

Patrick had to laugh. "Actually, Lt. Forestall, no worries there. I get seasick. That doesn't appeal to me at all."

Markham stared at him like he was a stinky piece of laundry. "No shit? You didn't tell me that."

"Does it make a difference?" Patrick asked.

"Dental school," Forestall said as he plunked down a large book and tapped it with his finger before Markham could reply. "We got lots of pathways to earn your D.D.S. or M.D. – shoot, you could go into public health and never have to ride a boat for your entire naval career!"

"I'm trying out for the SEALs," Patrick insisted.

"No, that's not up to you. The Navy decides who tries out for that gig. Only one out of a thousand is given the chance to try out. You're too big to be a SEAL."

"Ah come on, Forestall, you know that's not true," interrupted Markham.

"Look at me? I'm too tall—"

"Fuck sake, Forestall, you're too fat. Don't give him that line of crap," Markham continued. His face was turning red.

"Patrick, I think you and I better have our little chat in private, if you don't mind, LPO Markham."

It was one of those orders that Patrick understood should never be disobeyed, if Markham didn't want to get written up. He stood, patted Patrick's shoulder, and mumbled, "Meet you outside in a few. Remember what I told you."

Patrick rose out of respect. "Thanks, man. I won't be long."

Growling and without addressing Lt. Forestall, Markham left the room.

An hour later, Patrick was ready to leave the recruiter's office because Forestall refused to put in writing that he had a slot to try out for a Team. But before he could get out the door, the recruiter produced a request application, signed it, and Patrick was promised a consideration for a spot in the next class, which was due to start in six months. With that, Patrick agreed to report to Indoc later in the month, after he'd negotiated his separation from Tottenham.

Markham was pleased he'd managed to get the commitment his first time trying. "I've known guys that go back four, five times, and never get one. And then they have to fight all the way through basic. He must have understood you were serious."

"I am."

"You're gonna hate it. But it's worth it, in the end. I hope you don't hate me for encouraging you."

"That's a fair warning, but I'm ready."

STEPHANIE WAS TALKING to a girlfriend in Palo Alto

when Patrick entered their room. She was wearing the fluffy robe with the hotel insignia on it, her hair up in a clip, her long legs crossed sensually, showing off her red-painted toes. He put his paperwork on the edge of a side table and stared at it. Then he smiled up at her while she signed off the phone. So much was going to change for both of them. This would be the last lazy day they'd have, perhaps.

She untied the robe and floated over to him. His hands smoothed over the soft velvet of her skin, pulling her into his groin, enjoying her light fragrance and the warmth she emanated. Her fingers laced through his hair as she covered him in her warm breath. She didn't ask him anything, because she knew.

It hit him just before their lips touched that this was what he would be fighting for. This was what he would be coming home to. He also understood that in time SEAL wives sometimes soured to the whole gig. He hoped Stephanie's kisses and her body always remained soft and welcoming. He'd work hard to make sure it remained that way.

"Marry me before I go in, Stephanie. Would you do that for me?"

"Oh, sailor, you don't fool around much, do you?" She nibbled on his lower lip, pulling it with her teeth. "You like things fast. I can tell it's going to be an adventure. You're all about the adventure," she said as his hand found the juncture between her legs. "But I couldn't do that to my mom. She'd want the whole wedding thing. I'm afraid you're stuck with that."

He was enjoying the feel of her warm sex and how she jumped when he breeched her lips.

"How ever am I going to keep up with you?" She smiled, her eyes wide and sparkling, daring him further.

"Because I'll be there to carry you. You just keep up the kissing, and I'll do all the heavy lifting."

She squealed as he picked her up and threw her on the bed where he stood over her. She allowed the robe to fall to the sides. Lying on her back, she propped herself on her elbows and touched his groin with the toes on her left foot. "I'm going to make you work hard tonight, sailor. So get those clothes off, because I'm in desperate need, and you're the only one who can fill it."

TAKING HER TO the airport for the trip back to San Francisco was tougher than he'd expected. The happy banter was gone. Stephanie had been in near tears all morning, and her lower lip was drooping. He found himself unable to think of anything to say, for fear he'd make it worse. He knew the young girl he left behind when he went to England, but the woman sitting next to him now was still a stranger in many ways. She avoided his eyes. Patrick already felt the hole in his chest growing from when she'd disappear into the skies.

This is a consequence of us not taking it slow.

Her desperate kiss at the security checkpoint made him want to jump the line and join her. He was faced with the fact that the miracle of these few days in San Diego, the first of their real time together, was now ending. These would be the ones he'd think about when times got tough. They'd found each other after years of separation. They'd committed their lives to each other. They'd grieved together.

She wove her way through the line of passengers. She turned one last time to give him a brave smile and wave good-bye. When she disappeared around the corner to the gate, the building—which was bustling with people—felt cold.

They had a bright future, he thought as he drove from the airport after she was airborne. It could be long or it could be short, like her relationship with Ryan. However it turned out, he'd cherish every one of those days. He'd make sure she was never left alone again.

CHAPTER 13

STEPHANIE WAS EXHAUSTED when she landed in San Francisco. She took the train to the Palo Alto station, found her car, and was home less than ten minutes later.

Some of her flowers on the front porch had not been watered, as had been promised by the neighbor's teen. Someone had neatly tucked her papers on the wicker chair in the shadows, though. Mail had spilled onto the hardwood floor inside from the slot in the heavy oak front door. The little bungalow smelled musty, and she dropped her carry-on bag on her bed and took to opening up several windows throughout the house. Then she lit a vanilla candle.

A flashing red light blinked on her answering machine, and she was almost going to hit the playback but decided to take a few minutes to herself to assess what was going on inside her. She grabbed a glass of water and walked through the slider to her tiny backyard and inhaled the fall air. Leaves were turning brown, and several of her roses needed deadheading, sporting yellowing leaves. Her new persimmon tree was lit up in bright orange colors, doing its best to be bold.

Everything had changed in her life. She'd hardly had any time at all to float back down to earth after the uprooting Ryan's death created. Gray thoughts crept into her head like cobwebs, worrying her.

What have I done?

Was it loneliness that drove her into Patrick's arms like he'd wondered? She hadn't allowed herself to think about it when he was beside her, but now that she was alone and not warmed by his heat, neither smelling the intoxicating man-scent of his being nor hearing the steady beating of his brave heart, she wondered how strong she really was. Did she have what it took to keep up with this emotional roller coaster of a life? Because, she admitted to herself, that's exactly what it would be.

She texted Patrick to let him know she was back home safe. He told her he would call her later in the evening. He was arranging for his travel to meet up with the team in New York for the trip back to the United Kingdom.

Her home phone rang, and her mother's voice echoed throughout the kitchen from the answering machine.

"I left you three messages, Stephanie. Where are

you?"

Stephanie quickly snatched the phone up and shut off the recorder. She'd told her sister, Carla, that she was taking off for a few days with friends from school, since it was summer vacation. But apparently Carla hadn't relayed the news.

"I'm sorry, Mom. It was a last-minute trip with friends. I told Carla all about it. Since you were staying there, I just thought she'd tell you. But you're right. I should have called."

"Honestly, you girls are terrible about being in touch. You so busy you can't give your parents a call now and then?"

"Mom, don't start this. I *do* call. I just don't call every day." Her mother had a good friend who spoke to her kids daily. That had never been Stephanie and Carla's way. "I'm sorry she didn't tell you. It was very unexpected."

She kept her sigh quiet, but stared at the ceiling, wondering how much she should divulge of her new plans.

"Apparently. Well, I'm sorry we missed the service. We had a nice visit with the Rosens two days ago."

"Oh, that's good. How are they doing?"

"Well, you can imagine. Elaine looks like she's not slept in days, poor thing. We offered to fly them out to Florida for a few days to just get away."

Stephanie warmed up at her mother's nice gesture. The parents had all gotten along well during their pre-planning of the wedding. She was glad that would continue. "What a wonderful thing to do, Mom." She was having a hard time collecting her words and organizing her thoughts. It seemed unnatural to be talking about relationships from the past while she was looking forward to her new future, as if, somehow, she didn't have a right to be happy. And her mom would have all sorts of opinions about how soon she'd hooked up with Patrick. She was on the edge of overwhelm.

Well, dammit, she'd be right! Probably why I didn't call her and take the chance she'd pick up.

Would her mom understand someday?

"Are you and Dad still at Carla's?"

"Yes, but we leave tomorrow. Thought I'd try one more time to get hold of you. How about coming over for dinner tonight?"

"That would be nice. Are you sure she's inviting me?"

"Oh God, yes. Mrs. Rosen gave me a scare when she told me Patrick was there at Ryan's service. I thought for a brief moment you'd run off with him and eloped or something stupid like that."

Stephanie began to shake. It was going to be a very long evening.

Two hours later, there was a knock at her door, and a flower delivery man held two dozen long-stemmed red roses for her. She thanked him and brought them inside to add water and the preservative packet to the vase. The little card attached was covered in tiny, red velvet hearts.

Missing you already. You have every piece of me, Steph. Forever, Patrick.

She smiled and bet he'd taken a long time to come up with those words. She could just see him struggle with it all. She buried her nose in the velvety petals and brought them in next to her bed. Flipping the note between her fingers, she sat down and stared at them.

The flowers gave her courage—a sweet reminder that Patrick loved her, wanted to be with her, cared for her, and would do anything to make her happy. As the tears welled up in her eyes she vowed that whatever she was going to have to face tonight—or ever—she owed it to him, to herself, and even Ryan, to go on with her life, and to enjoy every day doing it. It was right that Patrick had come back into her heart. Aside from her bedroom discussions with him, he was the only man who could fill her with that love and tenderness she needed.

She deserved.

As she was on the way over to Carla's big home in the hills, Patrick called her. "Did I call late enough to find you naked?" he whispered.

She laughed. Even the sound of his voice was soothing. "Sweetheart, I wish. I'm on my way over to Carla's. Mom and Dad are still in town, but they're leaving."

"Okay. And how are you going to be with that?"

God, he knew her so well already!

"She already got a glowing report from the Rosins about how we were getting along, Patrick."

"Well, I don't know about anyone else, but the glow on your face was warm enough to power the whole house. I think it would be hard to overlook. You were, and are, so beautiful, even when you're sad, Steph."

She blushed, checking her face in the rearview mirror. The driver behind her honked when she didn't jump off the line when the stop light changed to green.

"And I owe you something special for those lovely flowers. They're right by my bed. I love the card, too."

"That was the hardest part! I held up the entire bus to the airport until I could finish that call. I got properly jeered too."

She smiled, excited she'd gotten it right. "What do you want for your something special?"

"How about you read me a chapter from one of those books you read?"

"Tonight?"

"Unless you want to do it now." He chuckled. "Our timing's a little off. We board the plane in an hour, and you'll still be there with your family."

"I'm open to improvising. Tell me what you'd like me to do, Patrick." She felt her insides clench as the familiar butterflies of new love lodged in her lower belly. She was wet with the memory of her big soccer player. Her chest was getting blotchy, and her bra felt too small for her engorged breasts and knotted nipples.

"I have this fantasy about you in all pink. I mean, I can't get it out of my mind."

She turned off the two-lane road and up the long winding climb to the top of the foothills. "Sounds nice. I'm wet. I have to keep my hands on the steering wheel, but oh man, if I could, I'd touch myself there."

"And I'd kiss it."

"I'd like that." She pulled to the side of the street, not halfway up the hill to Carla's. "So I've stopped the car. You want me to touch something pink and wet and warm for you?"

"Only if you won't get into trouble." His voice was low and gravely. "God, I got a boner the size of a nightstick."

"I love your nightstick, Patrick. And about getting into trouble, I want to get into trouble, but only with you. You call it, Patrick. I'm waiting. And I'm aching for you."

"Unlike you, I'm in a crowded gate area, and you're going to cause me to burst out of my jeans. So not fair."

"My tongue is lapping the underside of your big cock, Patrick. And I can taste the precum. Oh man, I think I still have a little of that left inside me. If I could—"

She sighed into the phone, slipped one hand under her skirt, and felt her stiff nub vibrating. She moaned.

"Jesus Christ!"

"Are you spilling like you did last night? Do you remember?"

"Oh, I can't think of anything but, sweetheart. I don't want to talk to you from the men's room, but in a minute, I'm going to have to. I'm scrunched up to the glass window here, and the guys are looking at me funny."

"I like that you're all turned on, and so am I. As a matter of fact, I'm having a little orgasm right now, sweetheart. And it is sooo delicious."

"Fuck!" he whispered desperately.

"Please. Fuck me, Patrick. I can't do what you do to my little parts down there. I'm going to get a vibrator, because I'm not going to be able to—"

"Now you've done it. I just came in my pants. Are you satisfied?"

"Are you?"

"Not nearly. But at least now I'll be able to sit

down."

"And you'll be sticky from New York to London. I think that's funny!"

"Oh, baby, I'm going to get so even with you. Next time I call, you be naked, and we'll do this right, okay?"

"You got it, future sailor. Tadpole."

"And you've cleared your calendar for at least an hour, so we can be private."

"Yessir. Your bidding I will do. Anything you want."

"I'm tempted to just dump the team and fly back out there to California."

"But think how horny you'll be if you wait, what? Two weeks? A little more? But we can have lots of fun on the phone, Patrick."

"I can't even look at the guys. I need a magazine, dammit."

She giggled her pleasure. "You could always take your shirt off and tie it around your waist."

"You're not helpful, Steph. I'm dying here."

"Well, just think how I'll be spending the next hour or two at Carla's. I'm going to tell them, Patrick."

"Of course you are. You're my girl. You'll always be my girl."

"I'll be the girl in pink. Maybe sometimes I'll be the lady in red!"

"I think that would work out just fine. I like the red

and deep rose parts of you. I love everything about you. Even though you are naughty and wicked and now I have to buy a new pair of pants."

"Well, if you must. I'm going to sit on Carla's dining room chair and pretend it's your face."

She hung up and with a chuckle, put the car in drive, and continued up the hill.

Her phone rang again, and she heard Patrick's soft whisper. "I'm going to love getting even with you. You forget I'm paid to play games. And I don't like to lose. You might as well surrender to me right now and give up."

"Gladly, my love."

"Okay, I'm off to find some pants. Love you."

"Love you more."

"Not possible." This time he hung up first.

Carla's huge driveway was filled with cars, indicating she'd invited several other people to dinner. Adjusting her skirt and checking her makeup, Stephanie smiled, musing how she could distract Patrick so easily. She wished she could see the scene live, but her imagination was pretty rich.

Carla met her at the door, holding a large goblet of red wine. "Sweetie! So glad you could come so last minute!" Her sister whispered, "Mom's been having kittens."

"How come you didn't tell her? You sort of got me

into trouble."

Carla looked behind her back to see if anyone was there. "I forgot. But then, she'd talked to Elaine Rosen, and I didn't want to add fuel to the fire."

"I disagree, Carla. I mean, I should have called her, but you didn't have my back."

Carla stiffened and took a gulp of her wine. She'd already had a lot to drink, Stephanie noted.

"Well, we just disagree. It was an innocent mistake. No harm, no foul."

She was dismissive and left the doorway, leaving Stephanie alone.

The dinner was noisy. Several of Carla's couple friends were present, but most notably, Carla's husband was not present. And she continued to drink. As the evening wore on, she entrenched into her chair and let the caterers do everything.

Afterward, Stephanie approached her sister, who was staring down at the table.

"Hey, I'm sorry if I came on rather strong, but are you okay, Carla?"

"Sit." She punched the chair to her right and then leaned forward. "First, Ray's having an affair with someone at the office. So I'm dealing with that."

"Oh, honey, I had no idea. Whe—"

Carla cut her off. "No, there's more. I'm afraid Ray's been overspending, and we may lose the house."

When Stephanie started to get up to give her a hug, Carla pushed her away. "Let me finish, please, and then you can have your say."

Her older sister did look horrible, not the bouncy life of the party she usually was. It must have been a sucker punch from hell. Stephanie had always thought of Carla as the more successful of the two. She made a good income working for a Silicon Valley firm, especially when compared to Stephanie's preschool salary, but apparently that wouldn't be enough to save her home. Ray was a prominent attorney in town and worked with several start-ups.

"Mom and Dad don't understand. I don't understand how, after nearly twenty years of marriage and two kids, I could be left nearly homeless."

"It can't be that bad."

"He took some client funds, Stephanie. They'll try to get it back any way they can, and if he's on the title, they'll take it. But he's gone through the savings, and the retirement, trying to right the ship, so to speak, so no one would find out. It's a sinkhole. I don't even know if bankruptcy will save me."

"You need to get some help."

"How? He knows every attorney in town!"

"That's not true. If he's doing this to you, he's crossed paths with someone else who'll love to take a piece out of him—without hurting you, if possible."

"Well, I just wish I could fly away—anywhere. Get away from all this."

"So, move into my place, Carla. It's tiny, but I won't be needing it much longer. If everything works out. Just for temporary. Some place where they can't hound you. It will be like camping for a bit, until you get your feet on the ground."

Carla's head bolted upright and she tried to focus. "What did I miss?"

Stephanie took her big sister's hand in hers and squeezed. "I know it's fast, but I'm going to move down to San Diego."

"San Diego?"

"Patrick is leaving soccer. He wants to try out for the Teams. And he wants me to move down there with him."

"You didn't."

Stephanie focused on their entwined fingers. Then she nodded her head, yes. "I did, Carla. I certainly did. I'm going to need your help with everyone—Mom, Dad, the Rosens. And I'll help you any way I can. But understand, Big Sis, if I don't take this chance, I don't think I'll ever be the same. I have to try to make it work."

"What if he gets—"

She could tell Carla didn't want to say the word. "He's just like Ryan. If I'm supposed to take a chance on him, how would it be if I didn't let him take his big chance too? What kind of a woman would it make me if I held him back from something he feels called to do? Would we ever make it if we took the safe road? I've looked and looked. There are no safe roads, Carla. Things happen, and then we move on." She sat up straight and removed her hands. "Just like you will. I *know* you will. There has to be something else out there for you."

CHAPTER 14

PATRICK'S HEAD COACH was angry. "You're throwing away a perfectly good career. You've barely touched the surface of what you can do here. And the money, you damn Yanks just don't appreciate the money. Not like some of these blokes who had to eat grass for dinner. Their millions mean a lot to them."

"And that's why my spot can be given to Adolphis or Riccio. It's a great chance for them."

Brian Sullivan had been a promising player, coming up through the youth leagues and playing in Germany and Holland before coming to Manchester. But in his second season, he tore up his knee so badly he was not able to be flexible and as fast as he was. He could still score, but he couldn't handle the ball with the speed and dexterity he once had. The big man put his arm around him.

"Ah, Paddy, yer breakin' me heart. The guys look up to you. You alone have started to disprove the theory that American players are sissies, pampered and way too soft. It's because you lot have choices some of us don't have here."

"Yes, Coach. I understand that. But I think this is what I was made for. If it doesn't work out, I'm not sure they'll let me out, but if there's a way to come back—"

"Fuck sake, Paddy. You'll fuckin' make those teams. You can do anything you set your mind to. I'm just pissed because I let you go to that funeral. You really ought to take some time and consider this carefully. Think about it for another year, or two. Then see. Who knows? Maybe you'll get injured, and—"

"And I wouldn't make the teams then. No, I want to go now. I'm healthy. I owe it to myself to try. Otherwise I'd never know. I got to do it for Ryan. He was like my brother."

Sullivan spat into the wastebasket in the corner, due to his habit of chewing tobacco. "It's a cryin' shame. Then you knock some little fucktard up, and you go home and get a job as a plumber and raise a dozen kids. It's all bad, Patrick. And for what? Not even for the money."

"I'd like to think it was for the honor. And just to see how far I could go."

"There comes a time when you give up Boy Scout things, Paddy. You got to grow up and be a man. Not everyone can jump out of airplanes or fight in places where they hate you. Hell, you could have that right here if you sat in the Manchester stands on game day. Wear the wrong jersey, and walk down the wrong neighborhood."

Patrick was chuckling and reached out to touch Sullivan on the shoulder. He was careful to make sure it was a manly tap. "Coach, I know where you're coming from. I'm going to do you and the team proud. I've been cultivating some bad habits. I'm about to set that aside and fly straight."

"So there's a woman involved. I can smell it sure as anything."

"There is."

"And you want to make this beautiful girl a widow then? Don't you think that's a mite cruel?"

"I've known her ever since grade school. She's the one. And she'll stand by me."

"Well, that's it then," Sullivan said as he threw his wet towel on the floor, hiked up his drawstring pants and began retying them. "When the heart goes one way, no amount of money can get a fella to go another." He looked up after he was done. "So make it count." As an afterthought he leaned into Patrick and winked, whispering, "And protect your hands in case you ever want to coach when you get tired of getting your ass shot off."

The Tottenham office efficiently processed his request, and his release became final once he paid off the balance of his contract. He was left with nearly a million dollars in his bank account, which would give him and Stephanie a nice nest egg to begin looking for a house.

Ronnie was in tears the last day of practice and could hardly look at Patrick. Even the late-night beers at the local pub didn't help.

"Just not going to be the same without you, Paddy."

"You'll get another roommate, Ronnie."

"Now I wish I'd agreed to retire after last year. I'm not going to lie. Gonna be a miserable year."

Patrick was going to miss Ronnie, too, with his opinions on everything from women to politics and occasionally that dangerous subject, religion. In all his gruffness, Ronnie made friends for life, and if you made the grade, there wasn't anything that would interfere.

Except leaving him behind. That was, Patrick was learning, an unforgiveable offense.

Patrick had offered to help train the young Nigerian boy, Adolphis, so he could take his spot. He gave the tall, lanky nineteen-year-old his backup pair of gloves and one set of his cleats, but he saved his long cleats and his brand new game shoes he just didn't have the heart to separate from. He tried to give the boy one of his green keeper jerseys, but the thing practically fell off his bony frame.

"You're gonna have to start working out," he instructed the boy.

"I work out," he said in his clipped English. "I run like the wind, and I can jump higher than anyone on our team."

"Yea, but you're a keeper. Remember that. You want to run? Go be a forward. The jumping's good but learn how to fall. You have to get some flesh on your bones so you don't break them next time some big German dude wants to hear the sounds of your skeleton shattering. You get pancaked, and you're done, Adi." He tapped his temple. "Be smart. Expect success, but plan for the worst. And you kick those guys if they come after you with their cleats up. You get their balls, and you ram them up to their necks, you hear?"

Adolphis grinned, his white teeth the complete opposite of his jet-black skin. "Yes, Boss. I can do that. I'll start drinking more beer."

"Thought all you Nigerians were Muslim? Besides, beer just makes you fat."

"No Man. I was raised in a missionary school, and I was the first of my family to learn to read. My father used to put the bible up on our shelf above the cook stove, just to prove that someone in his house could read in English."

"That's a nice story. He come to any of your games?"

"No, Man. All dead. It was called a religious cleansing. Burned my dad's bible. Then burned everything. Animals too. Nothing left."

"How did you escape?"

"I was playing football several kilometers away in the next village. My best friend, Mohamed, hid me with their family for three years. No more school for me. So, I played football. They helped me escape and come here."

Patrick was grateful for the conversation. "I had no idea, my man. Then this is perfect for you. This is your time to shine."

"And I have something for you, Patrick." Adolphis felt inside his backpack and came out with a tin foil package not more than an inch in size. Slowly, he peeled open the foil, revealing several tiny pages from a book, with the edges charred. He took two of the pieces and placed them back in the foil. The other two fragments of the book, he handed to Patrick. "This is for you. Part of my father's bible. I always thought if I stopped playing football, maybe someday I'd join the military and get those guys—I mean, *kill* those guys who wiped out the village, and my family."

Patrick didn't want to accept his gift, but Adolphis grabbed his wrist and held his palm up, placing the pieces of sacred text in the center. "You can be my spear. You go get the bad guys for me. And I'll protect your box."

The only thing Patrick could think to say was, "Deal."

CHAPTER 15

STEPHANIE WAS ABLE to find a new position in a combination preschool/Kindergarten right on the island. Carla and the girls helped her with the move and hung out at the beach for a few days before going home to Palo Alto. They settled in Stephanie's bungalow, and Carla managed to pay enough for rent to cover her payments.

Patrick was due back at Coronado within the week and had arranged to begin physical training with a couple of former SEALs who were either retired or medically discharged. Ryan's old LPO, Markham, was overseeing everything for Patrick until his team deployed. Stephanie was glad for his guidance, and she suspected that Patrick would have to earn his spot, but he'd get notes and useable suggestions to help grease the skids along the way.

Their telephone exchanges had kept up hot and heavy and, toward the time he was due to fly home, more and more frequent. She'd managed to find a local sensual shop, and though she was embarrassed the first time she went there, she discovered several other SEAL girlfriends were frequent shoppers. One had a part time job working there. She was looking forward to showing Patrick some of the devices she'd purchased.

At last, their reunion day was upon them. His towering frame and good looks made him appear more a movie star than a goalkeeper. He dropped his carry-on the instant he saw her and ran to pick her up, swinging her around.

"Man, I was going crazy on the plane. Never used to take that long to fly from London and New York. I think they've stretched the country."

Their long, sensual kiss drew a standing ovation from the deplaning passengers. "Welcome home, Patrick," she whispered to him privately, suddenly embarrassed about all the attention.

"How was the move? Did Markham and the other guys help out at all?"

"Carla and the girls helped tremendously. She didn't mind Ryan's buddies stopping by, either. It was really funny to see. The girls loved the beach."

"So, Ray's completely out of the picture?" Patrick asked while they waited, hand in hand, for the baggage carousel.

"I think he may be headed to jail. But I don't ask

for the blow-by-blow. For the first time in forever, my mom is actually staying out of it!"

"You hungry?"

She slipped to face him and made sure every part that could pressed into his frame. "I'm starved." Her hand slipped up to his neck, and she pulled his head down. He bent one knee and allowed it to massage her mound as she gasped.

"This is a pretty nice welcome. You must have been really bad," he growled and whispered back, pinching a nipple through her top.

"No, I'm a very good girl. Compliant. Willing to do anything for you, Patrick. I only want to be bad with you. But due to our differences in experience, you're gonna have to teach me." Her lips grazed his. She checked her surroundings, went up on her tip-toes, and slipped her tongue into his ear and whispered, "Sweetheart, I have some things you can use. You know, some of those things you heard buzzing in the background on our phone calls?"

"I say we skip dinner and go for dessert again."

"Good choice."

LATER IN THE week, they were introduced to several of the men on SEAL Team 3, who gave Patrick a hard time at first. He formed a special bond with Jameson Daniels, a young man from Nashville who had been a recording artist and had given up his singing career to join the teams. Jameson's wife, Lizzie, was from horse country in Kentucky, and the two became close. Stephanie helped their oldest girl, Charlotte, enroll in the school's third grade.

Jameson and Lizzie were frequent visitors to their little backyard firepit sessions. The four of them walked down the beach together and watched the sunset, allowing the girls to play in the sand and surf.

"What should I be asking about all this he's headed to? Any special coping skills I need to adopt?"

Lizzie pulled her hair from her face and gave her a coy smile. "I'm guessing you're good on the bedroom stuff. Funny how that takes care of so much other stress. If you can just be open and intimate, it helps. They come home with some horrible tales. Sometimes, you want them to tell you, so they can get it out, and often, I feel I could have gone my whole life without hearing it. But you do it for them."

"I hope he gets to be on Team 3. I think Jameson is a better influence than Markham."

"They say there never is any choice, but somehow, everything works out the way everyone who is important wants it. If Kyle and the other guys want him, he'll make the team."

"So, these bad stories, is that why the divorce rate is so high?"

Lizzie stared out at the ocean again. "They come home, and all they want to do is stay in bed, like they're exorcising their demons. I think some women take offense. We spend a lot of time fixing things around the house, even the car. We help each other. But then Mr. I'm-King-Of-Everything comes home and we're just supposed to drop our drawers and fuck until he feels right again."

"Wow." Stephanie wasn't sure how she felt about that. "That bad?"

Lizzie giggled. "No, silly. That *good*. I remember what Kyle's wife once told a bunch of us. *'No one will ever love you as hard as these guys do. It's a lot of work, but at the end of your life, you'll feel loved and needed, and they live to serve you right back.'* I think that's pretty freaking awesome, don't you?"

It was awesome. Stephanie hoped that the man who went off to the training would be the same one who came home. And when he returned from overseas, she could help him exorcise his demons and learn to pour out her heart like she'd never done before. That's when she realized that his calling was really her calling, too, and in order for it to work out between them, it had to remain that way.

That night Stephanie wore her brand-new red nightie and matching bright red fuzzy slippers. She changed out the white candles to red ones and sprinkled rose petals in the bathtub after drawing water. Patrick had been talking with Adolphis on the phone in the other room, which was something they were starting to do on a weekly basis.

She poured two flutes of champagne, set them beside the bath, crossed her legs, and waited for him with two candles in the far corner of the tub. Her heart was racing as she heard his footsteps coming down the hall.

"Steph—oh my!"

He'd stopped at the doorway and knew by now there was something special in the air. His head finally peeked around the corner of the door.

"Just what are you up to, little girl?"

She extended one of the flutes to him and shook her head. "Not tonight. I'm in red. I'm not a little girl. Are you ready for some fun, Patrick?"

His eyes sparkled, and she could measure the effect her play was having by the bulge in his pants. He tossed back the champagne in one swallow and set it on the floor nearby. His eyes roamed over her body, and it made her wet. She let him see her little shudder as her legs squeezed her sex and her areolas became knots.

He suddenly dropped to his knees, moved one knee over her other, and pressed her completely open to him. "I like this view better than the ocean at sunset, sweetheart."

She was burning up to have him touch her, but he just looked, angling his head and taking his time. At last she was so thirsty she finished off her champagne and dropped the flute to the floor.

"Tonight, we're going to use props. Bad things. Equipment. You do like your equipment, don't you, Patrick?"

"I like my equipment, but I like yours better. So you have been very, very bad. Is that what I'm seeing here?"

She nodded and widened her knees. He licked his lips and touched the petals on her sex. She rolled her head back, and she arched into a moan at the deliciousness of the anticipation. His thumb brushed her nub, and she gasped, moving toward his hand to press harder. After what seemed like hours, he lowered his head and washed her from stem to stern with his tongue.

He wrinkled his brow. "Cherries?"

She laughed, reaching for the bright red, penis-shaped lollipop behind her. She held it up and slowly allowed her tongue to drag the underside of the sweet candy, then put it deep into her mouth and pulled it out with as much suction as her lips could bring. It made a loud smacking sound.

"I don't think I've ever seen anything so beautiful. Well done, Steph. Only thing I worry about is, who's been teaching you all this stuff?"

"I have movies now."

He broke out laughing, which interrupted the mood slightly. She waited until he stopped without saying a thing, fixated on his eyes, placed the candy penis at her opening, and pushed it inside.

He was breathless and obviously in shock. His hand took over the reins, and he watched as the red candy coated her lips, her nub and all around her insides. Once more, with the candy still between her legs, he bent down and tasted her cherry lips, and once again, her body shuddered in pleasure at the sandpaper of his tongue.

She unbuttoned his shirt while he worshiped her sex, still on his hands and knees. She slid the collar and sleeves down his bulky shoulders and corded arms. Her fingers made quick work of the buttons on his fly. As soon as his cock was released she squeezed it, pulling the soft skin up and down while her thumb smoothed precum over his tip. He slowly rose, all six foot four of him, towering over her, breathing heavy as she took the candy from him. Setting it aside, she slid his pants down over his hips and came to her knees, lacing her arms up his thighs and cupping his balls.

He easily stepped out of his clothes just as she took him deep into her mouth. His fingers sifted through her hair, smoothing down her back over the red filmy nightgown, seeking the top of her butt cheeks. She worked on him in a slow rhythm, feeling him pulse, become more engorged, enjoying his man-scent, and enjoying how the muscles of his abdomen constricted. She pressed her breasts against his thighs, squeezed both butt cheeks hard, and took him in deeper…all the way down her throat.

Patrick pressed her face into him, needing her tongue and lips, whispering sweet little words of encouragement the harder she sucked.

He was going to explode. She reduced the tension, flicked her tongue against his tip, and felt him lurch.

"Oh, baby, you do any more of that and I'm done."

She giggled and drew her tongue along the underside of his cock just like she'd done with the candy.

"Oh man. I'm close, baby."

She stood, holding his balls in one palm. Not allowing their gaze to break, she removed her nightie and shivered in front of the man she loved, stepping just close enough that their thighs touched and her nipples burned across his upper abdomen. She slowly turned while he kissed her neck and allowed him to bend her over. She gripped the edge of the tub with the scent of the rose petals filling her nostrils. Very gently, he spread her knees apart and slipped himself into the soft peach of her sex, allowing her to feel every delicious inch of him as she inhaled. Once fully seated, he pulled out only to do it again.

Her knees got rubbery. He braced her by putting his palm against her tummy, holding her tight against his groin. He plowed deeper then slid his hands over her hips. He massaged her breasts as she leaned forward. "Is this the kind of naughty you had in mind, sweetheart?" he whispered in her ear.

"Oh, I have other things planned. We have another bottle of champagne, and other little delights."

He pressed against her cervix wall until she felt the dull pain of her own orgasm beginning.

"But I like how you take your time."

"Time? We got all the time in the world, Stephanie. We've only just begun." He rocked back. "You should see what I see, Steph. I got red cherry stuff all over my dick, but your white ass is a thing of beauty." He kissed her on her right shoulder, let his tongue make a trail to her ear, and whispered,

"Come for me, sweet Stephanie."

CHAPTER 16

THEY GOT WORD the BUD/S class was going to start up in three months, which was about half the time than they'd expected. That meant he'd have to go almost immediately to Great Lakes on the fast track Basic course for SEALs. They were waiting for that to come through, which could be any time.

Stephanie didn't want to pressure Patrick about their future plans, and she knew her mother and sister would give her hell for that, but he was preoccupied with his training workouts and several brotherhood getaways—which meant the consumption of lots of alcohol, ammunition, and skydiving. In fact, unlike most people's tastes, including her own, skydiving was just as good as surfing or lying on a beach on some exotic island to them.

So, even though they lived together and were affectionate and respectful, there were no lazy Saturday and Sunday mornings lingering around and getting into trouble. Their intimacy had suffered a bit. She didn't want it to slip any more.

Patrick studied the Special Warfare commands, read biographies, and asked lots of questions from his future SEAL brothers. One of her favorite things to do had been to sit across from him while he was engrossed in a book, wearing something very small and sexy, and read one of her romance novels. It worked nearly every time, but now even that had failed to get his attention as it used to.

She began to understand what Lizzie had told her about the difficulties of being a SEAL wife. But it niggled in her brain that he'd not mentioned anything about getting married, like he had two months ago, and although she told herself he was just preoccupied, it did worry her.

Now that his training was indeed really going to happen, she was left with two feelings side-by-side. There was the sense of urgency. If they didn't do it now, then they should not interrupt his training, which meant waiting a year and a half. The second thing that bothered her was that Ryan had asked her to marry him, and they *did* wait, so they could have had that fun honeymoon and the wedding for all the family.

Does a piece of paper and a ceremony mean that much? She knew he was committed. But she wanted his body every way she could, including legally. Just meant something that he'd take that step for her. But it wasn't the ten on her list of things.

Mostly, she decided to try to remove it from her mind. They had no time to plan anything. Would a quickie Las Vegas wedding work, like she heard others do? It just didn't seem respectful to do it that way for a piece of paper.

Watching Lizzie and Jameson together, and now more Lizzie than Jameson, didn't help much. Her parents were involved in their new life in Florida, traveling with a group of their friends. Carla's life was a complete mess with court appearances, attorneys, and the girls in tears frequently. It seemed selfish to try to put her needs squat in the middle of the drama and chaos that was her family.

Patrick came home from swimming in the inlet with Jameson, Cooper, Kyle and Jake's little brother Tyson. They had also included several other married men on Kyle's squad. None of the bachelors, especially Trevor Markham, were present. It had been an especially long and arduous workout, he told her.

He came out from the shower with the towel draped low across his hips. She had to look to see if he was loaded down below, and she wasn't surprised that he was. It was a nearly twenty-four-seven thing with Patrick.

But this time he noticed and gave her a smirk. She

pulled her book up to her face, crossed her legs on the bed, and giggled.

"Let's go down by the water and have some chowder tonight. Wanna do that?" he asked.

She was thrilled. "Sure!"

They found their favorite table behind glass on the large deck, next to a large gas heater. The sun was beginning to set.

"Never gets old, does it?" he whispered.

She noted how handsome he was in the glow of the orange sunset, how his pink lips were full. His smooth unbroken nose and shiny light brown hair waving in the breeze made him look five years younger than he was. But his huge shoulders and long arms, now filled out and tightened, signaled he was all man. He was in the prime of his life. He was almost graceful how he moved. She wished she'd seen him live play professional football.

"No, it never gets old," she agreed, not even glancing in the direction of the sunset.

"You want something else?"

"I'm good."

He left money on the table without waiting for the bill, took her hand, and led her down the steps to the sand and the pounding ocean beyond. An Asian youth waved as he ran past them, and Patrick returned the wave. They continued walking until they were close to the surf without having to worry about getting wet. A red cooler with a blanket draped over it waited right where he stopped.

She felt her heart begin to pump, lumbering so loud she was sure he could hear it. He wasn't looking at her, which was not normal. Instead, he bent over, picked up the old quilt, and spread it out, motioning for her to sit.

Of course, this had all been staged. A chilled bottle of champagne and two flutes were just ready for his steady hand and pour. He handed her the graceful stemware and tipped the rim.

"This is for you, Steph. You're my forever gal."

"And—" She got distracted when he pulled something from his pocket and held it in his closed hand. "What's that?"

"Drink, sweetheart. We both need a drink, I mean to say."

She was parched and nearly downed the bubbly in one gulp, as did Patrick. But her attention was still fixated on his right hand, resting in a fist on his right thigh.

He leaned forward, begging a kiss, and she did the same until their lips touched and slowly parted. He licked his lips. "You taste nice."

"You taste like champagne, Patrick." He held the bottle up with his left hand, which was *not* his dominant hand. She raised her glass and accepted the fill-up. "What's in your hand?"

He slowly looked down at his palm, extending it to her, "You mean this?"

It was a gorgeous multi-karat diamond ring surrounded by little diamonds. She'd never seen anything so huge before. Joy filled her.

"I asked you to marry me, and then I didn't execute the plan, did I?" he asked as he slipped it on her finger.

The size was perfect. She held her splayed fingers out to the deep rose horizon and remarked that it looked like it was made of light.

"Hearts On Fire, it's called. Some special cut. I had help picking it out."

She cradled her hand like it was a baby. "Oh, it's the most beautiful ring I've ever seen!"

"Don't I get a big kiss for that?"

"Oh. My. Gosh. Yes!" She leaned over to him, and he pulled her on top of him, climbing his hips. She placed her palms at the sides of his face and dropped to give him a proper, lingering kiss that made her so wet she wondered if he'd feel it.

He slid his long-fingered hands down her thighs, around to the backside of her jeans, then slipped them under her shirt, and found her nipples. She leaned over again and kissed his neck, moving to the front until she pulled his shirt out of his waistband. Lifting the cotton, she kissed him from his belly button to both his nipples, biting them one by one, before tucking her head under his chin and resting against him, listening and feeling his heartbeat.

He rocked her gently, neither of them saying a word, until she balanced herself on her forearms and traced the folds of his ear. "When do you want to do this?" she whispered.

"I got my orders to report to Great Lakes on Monday. I was thinking Saturday. What do you think?"

Although thrilled, she worried. "It will be impossible to find a place. Get things arranged."

He stretched his neck from side to side, and she heard a loud crack. "Ah. Better." He traced her lower lip. "I was thinking about something different than that."

"Like what?"

"Maybe a boat out there?" He pointed to the glistening dark blue water.

"Just the two of us?"

"Well, I think we'd better have a preacher, unless you'd trust a boat captain."

"My parents?"

"Will have to wait, sweetheart."

"No party?"

He drew a forefinger down her frontside and grinned. "Oh, there will be a party. Just not with witnesses."

Her eyes suddenly filled with water. "I didn't want to press."

"But you were smart to talk to Lizzie about it. Jameson got all over my ass, so good job. The guys said *if* I passed and *if* I was still in good shape, they'd not push to have me on Team 3 unless I cleaned it up with you."

"So that's how it works." She hadn't thought she'd divulged that much. "They tell you how many kids you should have?" She was teasing and hoped he took it that way too.

"Maybe, sometimes. If the guy needs it."

"Oh, that's awful!" She stiffened her spine and attempted to stand, but he pulled her back down on him.

"Whoa there. Hold on a minute. They don't do that for everyone. They fix things that need fixing. I needed fixing. They informed me I wasn't being fair to you, and if I didn't start paying attention, you'd tire of it." He held her hand, examining the ring. "Baby we don't ever want you to tire of this. I want you to be in up to your neck, like I am."

It wasn't tender, soft, pillow talk, but they were the sweetest words she'd ever heard.

On Saturday, Patrick borrowed a boat from one of the retired Master Chiefs on the island. They invited Jameson and Lizzie and a young youth minister from the local Presbyterian Church, who was all they could get with such short notice. The ceremony was brief, and Jameson played a guitar piece and sang a couple of stanzas from a new love song he'd been working on.

The five of them consumed two bottles of champagne and watched the ocean, but there was no food, no wedding cake and no dancing. Before he had too much to drink, Patrick brought the boat back and gave the Master Chief a wad of cash he tried to return.

They waved good-bye to Jameson and Lizzy, paid the minister handsomely in thanks, strolled hand-in-hand along the strand, bought an ice cream, and walked the six blocks to their rental.

And then the *real* party began.

The new Mr. and Mrs. Harrington enjoyed themselves immensely.

CHAPTER 17

PATRICK PASSED ALL the required courses for basic medic training, and since he'd been fast-tracked by some retired Lt. Commander in Coronado, a former Team Guy, and had orders to report back to begin BUD/S after just six weeks. He had never been so glad to get back to the sunny coast of San Diego and to resume just a few days of normal life with Stephanie before the tough stuff began.

As was common with the men on Kyle Lansdowne's squad on SEAL Team 3, before any big deployment, they held a bonfire at the beach and invited all the wives and girlfriends and kids. Not all girlfriends could come, of course. It was strictly a family affair.

Patrick stood with Kyle, Jameson, Coop, and T.J. Both Coop and T.J. were medics on the team, and he hoped to be mentored under one or both of them some day.

Most the squad was moving out next week for a short TDA back to Baja California where they'd been instrumental in rooting out a small family cartel of human sex trade traffickers. One of the complications on a recent mission was the promise that one of Kyle's men would marry the daughter of a Mexican general who helped them escape. Part of the bribe also included the gift of a bright red Tesla, courtesy of Uncle Sam's Treasury Department. The guys were recalling stories about seeing the general streaking across the border showing off in his aloha shirts and racking up speeding tickets they had to get expunged.

"How'd you get wrapped up in that one?" Patrick asked.

Coop was wearing shades, even though it was dark out. He raised his glasses on his forehead and leaned into his LPO. "How do we get into these things, Kyle?"

"You don't want to know the half of it, Patrick. Stay a virgin. You'll see enough action when you get pinned. You wouldn't believe any of us with some of the stories we've got to tell," said T.J.

"It was that damned Jake," Kyle said, pointing his beer at a couple roasting marshmallows with a bevy of red-headed girls fluttering around them getting sticky. The dark-haired SEAL waved back, oblivious to what had been said about him.

Patrick knew it would take years to get up to speed,

so he asked, "Who's going to marry the girl?"

"I'd promised her to Ollie, but he's not coming this time." Kyle smiled and clinked beers with the rest of them. "Gents, I think we better figure that one out before we get down there."

"We got a handful of single guys going. Some of the married ones might not mind, either," said T.J. "She's a hot little thing."

They all laughed.

"So, Patrick, we sort of broke the rules here tonight with you, but you were tight with Ryan, and you took over his girl, and we like that in this crowd. You listened and got yourself hitched, and you managed to get out of Great Lakes without being recruited for Dental School," Kyle began.

"Oh, they tried."

"They always try. Always the same. The Navy has the worst dentists in the whole fuckin' world," said Coop. "Sometimes, they just call you in and take a perfectly healthy tooth and put a crown on it, and there isn't anything you can do about it."

"They redo fillings that are brand new, and then they fall out so they get to do it again. Stay away, Patrick. Trust us," added T.J.

Patrick scratched his chin. "I got a small fortune in dental work. Most my teammates on the Spurs were missing their upper teeth. Occupational hazard."

"Not like rugby, huh?" said Jameson.

"Well, old footballers go play rugby, if they're built for it. Big guys that can't stop playing and love the mud, the blood and the guts. Gotta chase the adrenaline. If they didn't lose their teeth before, rugby will do it."

"So finish your story, Kyle. You're getting a little hammered, I think." Coop punched Kyle in the arm.

Kyle delivered a wide grin. "Okay. So we never have anyone who hasn't been through the ceremony come here. Wives of fallen guys and the kids can come of course, but I mean you're an exception, Patrick."

"I'm honored."

"And we're here to give you a little advice since we won't be here when you have your first little cut or scrape, and we won't be there to talk you down from quitting." Kyle took a deep breath. "So here it is, the secret." He looked at the other SEALs, and together, they shouted,

"Don't quit!"

Patrick chuckled. He'd told Markham and Ryan's mates on Team 5 the same thing. Because he got it from Ryan.

"You mean all those videos I've been looking at about conditioning, mental attitude, and stuff is crap?"

"Most certainly crap. You walk in there with a plan, a system, and boom, you're the first one out," said

Coop.

"They're going to get under your skin. They'll call you pretty boy, 'cause they know all about you."

"Because of Ryan."

"Yes, and the other little job you had," Kyle said.

"Don't pull attitude with any of the instructors there. They called me the Elvis SEAL," said Jameson. "Pissed me off."

"They're looking for you to be able to take it. Not get upset. Go along with the program, don't complain, don't brag, and just keep your head down. Don't look at them or engage. You want to be invisible, man, or they'll pick on you." Cooper followed it up with a half-smile. "You'll be fine. Are you scared yet, kid?"

Patrick said no, but his legs were shaking.

BEFORE THEIR CLASS got to Phase I the dropout rate was twenty-five percent. Ryan had told him about the row of blue or green helmets he'd see every morning before they began, the ones that used to belong to his former classmates. He knew about the little rubber boats and the sharp rocks, the telephone poles they had to carry in teams, and the timed swims in the murky inlet floating with garbage and oil. But unlike Ryan, Patrick got to go home at night except for trips to the gun ranges at the Nevada desert. Before he was done, they'd been to Alaska, Mexico, Canada, Nevada, Texas and even Florida.

The instructors gave him a heads-up on what to be prepared for sometimes, which really saved him. He'd wear extra socks or thermal underwear, tended to his cuts and blisters carefully, and made sure he got as much rest as possible when he was off.

By the time Hell Week arrived, he'd already lost twenty pounds.

He came home at different times of the day or night. Sometimes, Steph had made a nice dinner or expected him to take her some place and he just didn't show up and couldn't call. She tried to make his favorite meals, but he didn't want to be fussed over. Little things would bug him. Most of the time, he just remained quiet because arguments, and there were only a few, really messed him up mentally the next day.

He forgot her birthday, as well as his mom's, which was nearly unforgiveable. He was up in Alaska running in the snow with backpacks filled with rocks during Christmas. One of the guys in the class had a baby during the training, and he was allowed to leave for one night, but came back the next day.

Jake's younger brother, Tyson, became his swim buddy. They teamed up for their timed swims. Tyson had had some formal coaching, so was a great help teaching him how to turn and kick and extend his arms, so he could move through the water faster.

Patrick's stamina was better from his years of soccer, but the subtle techniques made a tough job a lot easier. Those were the little things he looked for.

He made a habit of not talking about what he was going through, because mostly, it was the same thing, day in and day out. But when Hell Week was going to start, he let her know.

He'd been lying on his back, staring up to the ceiling when he told her. She probably had not been sleeping, either, because she slipped warmly to his side. It felt good, and he realized he'd missed being intimate with her.

"I'm sorry I've been so preoccupied, Steph. You've been real good, honey. Thanks for not bugging me."

Her hand grazed over his chest, and she kissed him there. "I know you're doing what you were made for. I don't want to interfere. I can handle it, for a while."

She reached down and massaged his cock, her soft perfume wafting around him, reminding him of what was on the other side of all this training and what he was doing this for.

She let him take her without a lot of foreplay, and he buried deep, loving the warm feel of her acceptance of his hard body. He wanted to hear her crash and burn before he came, and she was working up to it, but struggling. He unwrapped her legs from around his waist and drifted down, putting his mouth on her pulsing sex. He worked on her until she started mewling like a kitten.

He pressed her legs up over her head, her knees hugging her ears, and drove in deep. Spreading her buttocks, pressing her nub with his thumbs, and holding her little ass tight, he completed his penetration to climax. When he was done, he was drenched and out of breath.

He kissed her goodnight and found she'd been crying.

"What is it, sweetheart?"

"Nothing." Which meant there was something after all.

"Tell me."

"Do you love me, Patrick?"

"Of course I do." He bent down and pushed away her tears. "Did I hurt you?"

"No. I'm just—"

He could see her large brown eyes in the moonlight, staring straight at him with her innocence, her gentle love for him written all over her face. "I guess I'm a little bit lonely."

Patrick didn't want to hear that. Not tonight. Not the night before he was to start Hell Week. He rolled onto his back and closed his eyes, trying to think of a way to explain how he just couldn't do this. He just couldn't get there to connect with her in any way but physically. That part, the sex, was always great. But he knew what she meant.

"It won't be long now. Hell Week, and then I think it gets easier. Maybe we can celebrate afterwards. But until then, Steph, I gotta be tough as nails."

He recalled how a couple of the recruits had gone out drinking the night before a training they hadn't expected and the whole group of five had to drop. He didn't want that to be him.

Then he remembered what she'd asked him.

I'm such a stupid fuck!

He leaned over and pulled her chin to the side to face him. "Steph, I love you more now than I ever have. You're the one I come home to, honey. Hang in there with me for a bit, and I'll get back to being me again, if I can. I'll be honest with you, so far, I've done pretty good. This next week will test me in ways I never knew it would. I want to be ready for it."

She stroked his cheek, gently kissed him on the lips. "I know, Patrick. But thanks for saying it. Maybe next week or the week after we can sit down and talk about stuff I want to do, stuff that's important to me, honey. Okay?"

His veins were beginning to perk up, and now he might have trouble sleeping. He knew he should not ask her, but he did anyway.

"Like what?"

She hesitated for a second and then rubbed her forefinger across his lip. "I want to have your baby, Patrick."

IN SPITE OF the distraction, the curve ball she'd thrown him, he made it through Hell Week. He'd never felt so much pain in his life, and he was bleeding in places he didn't think he had blood. He came home with the green feet, just like Ryan had, from wearing shoes soaked with saltwater for six days straight. He was wet the whole time, trying to stay awake on the beach, letting the surf creep up and claim him like some frosty witch. On top of it, the week was rainy, unusual for San Diego, as if the angels themselves were crying. The coughing, vomiting, moaning and the sound of men dropping, falling in the sand to try to reach that damned bell mounted to the back of the truck they had to ring to quit made him feel like he was part of a prison population. Not a valued asset or elite warrior.

He kept seeing Stephanie with her belly enlarged and replaying that conversation he now regretted. The "not now, Steph," words he'd said probably a little too harshly. But he didn't want to think about being a caring, loving father to anyone. He didn't think he'd be very good at it, especially now. They'd never talked about kids because he'd grabbed her and pulled her down to Coronado so quickly. Now all his second thoughts were swarming around in his head, making him crazy.

Fuck!

What was so upsetting about her words? She depended on him, and he was okay with that. But creating another person, someone who would be connected to him forever and forever, someone who was totally defenseless and would not survive without his constant care, it was too much to think about. He wondered if he'd ever be. And that would be a huge problem for Stephanie.

As he shed his clothes, she wasn't home that day. There was no little celebration that night. He left everything at the foot of the bed, took a quick shower, and crashed naked across the mattress, waking up later on to cover himself. And Stephanie wasn't home.

In the morning, he made his own coffee. The house was bright and cheery, and he resented it. He sat in the living room and turned on the TV but didn't even look at it. He drank his coffee like a zombie and made another cup.

He found her note on the kitchen counter.

Gone to Palo Alto to be with Carla. I'll be back Sunday.

Well, he passed one test but flunked another. He remembered what the men had told him and realized that yes, he had to fix it.

He thought he would be happier. Wasn't this what he wanted? Where were the cheering crowds? He'd saved the game.

But he was playing to an empty stadium.

CHAPTER 18

STEPHANIE WORKED TO keep her emotions between the lines, remembering all along what Lizzie and other wives had told her. She decided to give Patrick some space. She knew he would make the BUD/S cut. But his comment before he left for the week-long ordeal had left her wondering if they'd make it as a couple.

Carla's life was a mess. She was glad she could give a shoulder to her big sister.

"Ray's trial is wrapping up." Carla said as she puttered in the kitchen.

"Well, that's good. You've got to be pleased it will be all over soon."

"Each week, I get served with more papers. Bills, demands from attorneys. He's such a shit." She put her hands on her hips and wrinkled up her nose. "What the hell did I ever see in him?"

"He's handsome, I guess. In a wolfish way," Stephanie said softly. With his pointed canines that appeared to be filed to a point, he'd always reminded her of a werewolf.

"Oh, thanks for that."

"You know I never liked him. I don't know what you were thinking. You're a working fool, Carla. He took total advantage of you."

Carla sighed and polished a glass before putting it away. "My counselor says there's always a payoff. People don't stay with horrible people or in horrible situations unless there's a payoff somewhere." She threw the dishtowel on the countertop. "I just can't remember what mine was."

"So, you got some help?"

"Attorney? Yup. Our CEO has a friend he graduated at Stanford with. He's awesome and very well respected. Turns out, he knew all about Ray before I had to elaborate."

"Well, that's good. How are the girls?"

"That's the part that sucks. They still want to see him, that asshole."

"Well, he's their dad."

"You'll be very proud of me, Stephanie. I told them they better start studying and working on their soccer, because if they wanted to go somewhere good, they were going to have to get a scholarship."

Carla's youngest was only eight, and Stephanie

knew how that would go over, but she kept her mouth shut. "I think it's good that they earn their way. Not have it handed to them."

Her sister didn't acknowledge the comment. "How's Patrick? Married life?" It was the first time Stephanie saw a smile on her face. She wished she'd had better news.

"Complicated. He's under a lot of stress with the training."

"Duh! God, what those guys go through."

"True, and I was warned."

Carla's radar kicked in. "Tell me."

In spite of what she'd told herself on the drive up, she was unable to keep the tears from spilling over and running down her cheeks. "We had a—I don't know what to call it now—a disagreement or something—I don't know."

"About what?"

She wiped her face with the back of her hand, grabbed a tissue, and blew her nose. "I told him I wanted to get pregnant. It wasn't the right time to discuss something like that."

"Bull shit it's not! You guys are married. Babies come when you're married. Don't you remember those stories? *'You'll have a baby when you really love someone'*—like it was some magic spell or something. Remember us whispering about it after I learned the truth?"

Stephanie laughed. "I do remember that night. You showed me the pictures. I couldn't make any headway with them. And then I had to open my big mouth at breakfast the next morning, right?"

Carla mocked her little girl voice, "'Mommy and Daddy, what does fuck mean?' That messed up their oatmeal big time. That was so funny! I told all my friends at school. It was the topic of the day."

"I'm having a hard time finding my way. And although Lizzie told me I might take a back seat, now that it's happened, I don't like it much."

Carla ran to her side and gave her a hug. "You have to be able to talk about everything and anything. You can't keep something like that stuffed inside."

"You're right, but I should have seen it sooner and done something about it. A few weeks go by, while he's so totally focused, as he should be, on making it through the qualification, and pretty soon we're not having sex, not talking, not being warm to each other. It scares me, Carla."

"Stephanie, stop being a snowflake. Put your big panties on. The guy is nuts about you. You gotta quit being afraid of him. I can't understand why you're acting this way. You're not afraid of anything!"

"I don't want to lose him."

"No, you're just being too young. You have to grow up. He's a man—a high action man—doing all sorts of incredible things other men watch on TV with their popcorn. He's out there trying to live that adventurous life. You gotta keep up with him, Steph."

She loved her sister, but hated when she was right. She picked her phone up from her purse and was about to call him when Carla wagged her finger.

"Nope. You get your little butt back to San Diego and do it in person. You have one of those little conversations that winds up in real steamy sex. That will fix anything. Trust me, I do know that. If I can make it fifteen years with the wolfman, you can charm the pants off that Adonis. You've got a man who will love you stronger and longer—"

Stephanie giggled. "Stop it."

"I'm serious. It isn't the sex, but that will bring you together. Don't let it drift off. Make it vivid, real. And make it so he can't get away from you. You take him by the balls and let him have it. You walk around naked and let him see what he's going to miss if he doesn't get himself good and hard and service you *right* away. That's the attitude you need!"

"I always knew there was more of Mom in you than in me," Stephanie said between her laughter.

"Nothing like ten years of deprivation to bring out the cougar in me. Any one of those young SEALs would do just fine. And you're surrounded with them. Lord Almighty, woman, get a grip!"

SHE WAS ABOUT a hundred miles to Coronado when her phone rang.

"I've been a dick."

She listened, enjoying the sound of his pain.

"I'm sorry, Steph. I got wired up too tight. Almost blew the last day and chucked it all in."

"But you didn't."

"Of course not."

"And you passed?"

"I did." His voice got low and gravely. "And I kinda need a nurse."

"I can do that. I do that really well, Patrick. But can you do something for me?"

"What?"

"Can we at least talk about whether or not you want a family—not now—but some day? I just need to know. I never thought you'd be resistant to it."

The long pause had her apprehensive.

"Are you okay?" She listened and couldn't hear anything except the sound of his snoring.

SHE WALKED INTO the house and found him still asleep on the bed with the phone in his hand. He had sores that were beginning to scab over at the tops of his thighs and under his arms and some deep scratches and chaffing on his inner thighs. She had calculated he'd been home less than a day, but already he was healing.

She found some first aid cream and began to apply it to some of his weeping areas. He'd showered, and the sores weren't infected, but until they scabbed over, he'd be very uncomfortable. Patrick stirred and then grabbed her wrist just as she was about to apply more cream.

"I'm just trying to help make you better, Patrick."

"I appreciate that. Best thing for it would be a dunk in the ocean, but no cream, okay?"

"Maybe a warm bath?"

He released her wrist and smiled at her. "Now you're talking."

"Come on. Get your fanny up and into the tub, then. I don't want to have to look at you this way, or I'll start to hurt too."

He pretended to let her help him up, but he was doing most of the work. She left him at the bathroom doorway while she drew water in the tub. From behind, she heard his whisper, "Nurse, you have the finest ass I've ever seen."

She blushed and turned to face him. "Really? And just what do you intend to do about it?"

He walked toward her, all six-foot-four of naked eye candy. "Well, first I'd remove that constrictive device that's holding those lovely orbs. I'd release them." He slid a palm down her thigh and then around to her rear. "I'd get you out of that uniform you're wearing, and I'd go get some cherry lollipops, and I'd get you into trouble." He kissed her beneath her right ear. "I might even get you fired."

"Fired or fired up?" She threw her arms around his neck, slipped off her shoes and jumped to wrap her legs around his hips. "Does that hurt?"

"I can't tell. I took a pain pill."

She smiled and undulated into his lower abdomen. "So you can't feel a thing, then?"

"I can feel that."

She rubbed her lips across his and then bit him playfully on the lower. "I can heal you, Patrick, but you got to let me."

He let her slide down his front, placed his palms beneath her jaw, and kissed her long and lovingly. "I've been a fool," he said when they came up for air.

"Yes, you have."

"I'm going to make it up to you, and in return, will you heal me?"

"I'll think about it."

He touched her cheek with the back of his hand. "You will make a beautiful mama someday, and I want to have babies with you, Steph, as many as you want. But not right now, honey. We'll do it when I can be a proper father, not when I'm trying out for the team." He kissed her.

She nearly fainted in his arms.

CHAPTER 19

PATRICK GOT HIS Trident one sunny Sunday afternoon in late Spring. The Navy asked Kyle Lansdowne to give the address. Stephanie sat with his parents in the front row. A whole line of SEALs he knew well sat two rows behind and were especially loud when his name was called, and Kyle got to pin the Trident to his chest. Most of the audience turned to see who was making such a fuss.

When Tyson got his Trident, the whole band cheered again. Jake, unfortunately, was on deployment and couldn't see his brother graduate. Tyson and Patrick took a selfie of the two of them and they sent it to him. He was in a training with the Norwegian Special Forces, the FSK. Jake sent them back a picture of the inside of his mouth and then a picture of a new mermaid tattoo he'd picked up in Norway.

Although Patrick was now a SEAL, this was the beginning of his qualification training, which would take several more months. At the end of that time, he'd be joining SEAL Team 3, he'd been told.

In the next few weeks after the ceremony, the graduates separated. Some went to the burn center in Texas. Some went to language school in Monterey, and others did a tour in Virginia and Washington, at either the Pentagon or Quantico, depending on their career trajectory. Though he was going to train as a medic, they elected not to send Patrick to the long course in North Carolina. Instead, he was informed he'd be working up with SEAL Team 3 for an urgent mission to Central Africa.

Several weeks ago, Patrick had told Kyle and the rest of his soon-to-be teammates about the keeper he'd trained and left behind in England. So, when Kyle asked him to reach out to his former teammate, he suspected it had something to do with where they were being deployed.

"Yup. Somewhere in the Nigerian theater, depending on the need and the safety of the insertion. The Head Shed is working out the deets now," Kyle told him.

"Any idea when?"

"Soon."

It had been "any day now" for nearly two weeks.

"Be careful, Patrick with that phone call. And if anyone asks, I didn't request it, okay?"

"Got it."

He trusted Kyle to reveal the source of the information if it was necessary and he also agreed not to discuss it with the others until the time was right.

Throughout the year and a half since he'd left Tottenham, he'd called Adolphis at least once a month. The young Nigerian keeper was having a great year and had found that rhythm with the team that brought with it magic and success. Patrick explained to Stephanie that people called it *The Beautiful Game*, which had originated with the fans in Brazil decades ago. When everyone did what they were supposed to, it looked like a graceful, choreographed dance. The team would scatter, like specs of oil in water, and then they'd come together to ram through their opponent's defenders to get to the box. He explained that if it was done right, the pattern resembled one pulsing organism working in harmony, anticipating passes and plucking things from the air like a multi-tentacled beast.

He found a quiet spot in the backyard and dialed the Nigerian keeper.

"Paddy! Does this mean you made it?"

"I did indeed. I'll send pictures of my uniform."

"Oh yes, we want to see all the equipment. You've done well."

"Say, what's the name of that village you're from, Adi?" Patrick asked.

"Tengo. In the north. But I don't think it exists. Why? Are you going there?"

Patrick didn't want to lie to him, but he was not allowed to reveal where they were to be traveling. "We're doing some studies of militant groups, and I thought I'd just see if there was any activity I could reference for you. We're half a world away."

It wasn't a lie, because they were still in California. While Adolphis was describing the area, the mountains he used to run in, the lake he slept next to as a little boy, reading his treasured books, Patrick located the village on a map, and discovered it was right in the middle of a large red zone, meaning it was covered and fully saturated with militant groups of all kinds.

"You coming over here for a visit soon? The team wants to see you. They want to know if you've been to the White House yet." His laugh consisted of breathing in, instead of blowing air out, which gave it a strange animal sound that could be rather scary. More like a croak.

"Funny. No, we don't visit the President. He has his own people. We swim in the ocean and sun on the beach, that sort of stuff."

"And you would be pullin' my leg, too, Paddy." Adolphis couldn't make a soft *D* sound, so pronounced his name like it was spelled Paw-**Dee**.

"Well you know how they say, if I told you, I'd have

to kill you."

"Excepting that you have to catch me first, Paw-Dee. You forget, I can outrun a giraffe! I'm faster than the wind itself."

"Now look who's pulling my leg. Are you sure they aren't using you as a forward?"

"Dos guys are great with the ball, but they've been shit with the overkicks. Coach says he buyin' ebrybody glasses with their bonus money if dey don't start getting them in the box. I can score better than they can."

"Well, there you have it. You're going to get good fast if you're having to do all the defending. If they can't shoot—"

"I know, I know, if they can't shoot, they can't fuck," Adolphis blurted out.

Patrick laughed that Adi had remembered the story about General Patton serving in North Africa, who used to tell people he didn't mind women, even professionals, to travel with his troops. '*If they can't fuck, they can't fight*' was one expression that had endeared him to his men. Patrick adjusted it slightly to use in the context of playing soccer, and his coach and the team loved it. So, if players were missing, it meant things at home were bad.

"No dos guys, they fuck okay. Bunch of strange guys from some little country near Russia. Little guys, you know?"

"Geez, I thought they'd take the money from my contract and get some decent players," said Patrick.

"Oh, they're good players. Run their little legs off, but they make me laugh. Coach says they drink too much. That's alright, I guess. But they have these little legs. So fast, but you can't see their feet they go so fast. They fall all the time."

"They're supposed to do that. Drawing fouls."

"They stumble over themselves. Not pretty, Paw-Dee."

"Maybe they just need a chance to learn."

"I know what it's like to come to a foreign country. I thought everyone spoke English, and at least I knew that. But these guys don't. And they're getting so confused with the side of the street, you know? One guy nearly got hit by a bus, Paw-Dee. He was looking the wrong way."

Patrick didn't know at first what he'd been talking about and then realized they were getting confused driving on the left-hand side of the road.

He reminded Patrick that the group leader had the lion tattoo on his cheek. "You find dat guy, you be my spear, Paw-Dee."

"Well, that's not likely, but I'll take it with me wherever I go, and I'm taking your father's bible with me too."

"Good luck. It will bring you safety."

"Well, it already got me through the training without injuring myself. So, Adolphis, you take good care of yourself, and those keeper gloves I gave you."

"I only use those for game days. Thank you."

He told the Nigerian keeper that Stephanie was well. Her profession as a teacher, even a teacher of little ones, gave her high marks in his book. They said good-bye and promised to talk in a month or so.

The squad was ordered to report to the Team building at four in the morning and to bring their gear. Patrick took time to say good-bye to Stephanie, who was having difficulty showing her courage.

"Steph, don't think about it. Just go on with whatever else you regularly do. I'll be home before you know it." He tucked her head to his chest and rubbed the back of her head, feeling the hot tears soaking through his shirt.

At last she looked up at him. "I'll be okay. I think the first one is the worst, or that's what Lizzie told me. We're going to spend a lot of time together and boost each other."

"Good idea, sweetheart. Lizzie's strong. You can help her out with the kids too."

"Will you be able to contact me during—" She welled up and placed her hand over her mouth.

"Hey, you have to remember, I'm with the baddest

motherfuckers on the planet. I'm a newbie, and they aren't going to let me do dumb stuff. There will be lots of eyes on me this first time, just in case I run into something new or forget something I was taught. I have total confidence in these guys."

She reluctantly nodded and allowed him to slip away. Before he walked out the door, he stopped and rubbed his belly and then pointed to her. "We'll talk about getting you fat when I get back. Deal?"

"Deal," she said with a thumb's up. She ran to him one more time, clutching his shirt tight, and then nearly pushed him out the door.

THE BRIEFING WAS interesting but brutal. Pictures of decapitated women and children piled up along the road or in shallow ditches were flashed on the screen. Kyle let the State Department liaison go over the locations of several bands of warring factions.

"Problem for us is that they've got a weak government. They can't protect all the people, so we have these warlords springing up that take the place of what the government can't do. And then you have the religious zealots who want to make this into a Holy state governed by their laws. They're not interested in ruling the people. It's submit or die."

Kyle added one point. "You're sitting there asking yourself how come the people don't rise up. They have no means. They aren't armed with anything but farming implements. The men can't protect their women or children. So they are recruited to go off with these gangs. The crops aren't tended to or get overrun. They have no way out."

Coop raised his hand. "Can I ask a question?"

The liaison nodded at him.

"Can you tell me why we're there?"

"That's on a need to know basis," barked Lt. Commander Ashcroft, who had been standing in the shadows.

"We also got Ebola happening. That's why everyone got shots last week," said Kyle.

The liaison pointed out that the death toll this year alone had exceeded thirty thousand. The room was filled with whistles and grumbling.

Someone said from the back row, "So why don't we let the Ebola just wipe them all out? It would be a hell of a lot cheaper."

Patrick knew that wouldn't be well received, but every man there was thinking the same. It would take a lot of cases of the disease before the death toll would scratch the surface of what the armed conflict had caused.

Lt. Commander Ashcroft answered him tightly with the facts. "Because, son, we don't want them weaponizing the disease. They'd send infected people all over the continent, perhaps into Europe or the States, just to start wholesale panic. We don't want to give them that chance."

"And we don't let innocent people die," added Kyle.

The liaison flashed a picture on the big screen. The dark-skinned man had a chubby face, well-trimmed beard, and a dark green tam atop his head that was part of his green and tan uniform. Behind his dark glasses, Patrick bet his eyes would have revealed a well-trained killer. It was hard to miss the tattoo of a lion on his left cheek.

"Johnathan Fortune, although we don't think it's his real name. This is the most dangerous guy in the country. He runs rogue to all the clerics and indiscriminately kills people of all religious faiths. He's nearly single-handedly wiped out the entire Christian population in the north. He was serving prison time before the new regime took over in 2000. He's been a busy boy. We think he'll either unite or wipe out the other warlords within the next couple of years.

"The government is weak, and we're trying to shore that up, but there's only so much we can do. Our aid packages have been intercepted. These guys have even learned how to hack into the State's banking system and have stolen millions from the government. We don't want to send troops, if we can help it. We need you to bring this guy to justice."

The room hung silent. Did this mean he was to be kidnapped, brought to the States, or killed?

The liaison waited a sufficient length of time before he explained. "First, we want his papers and want to know where he's getting his help from. We have ideas, but we need to know. And second, we need for the people to see that even Johnathan Fucking Fortune can be brought to justice. We're planning a public trial in Nigeria, or at least that's the plan."

As Patrick climbed aboard the wide-gut transport plane for Norfolk, strapped in, and stowed his bags at his feet so they didn't interfere with the next man's, he was still seeing those visions of the villagers massacred. They'd showed him films of torture and killings before. But the pictures of the small children—kids like Adolphis, just wanting to play soccer and have a decent life—brutally murdered before they even had a chance got to him.

Inside his jacket pocket, he fingered the tiny wad of tin foil he'd used to cover the page fragments he'd been given. He did hope that they'd keep him safe. He wanted to come back to Adolphis someday and tell him that he'd been one of the spears who got this cretin and that the bastard wouldn't be murdering any more of his country's youngsters.

CHAPTER 20

A NEW SCHOOL year was upon the Coronado Shores Charter School, where Stephanie was beginning her second year of teaching. Several of the older students had been in preschool for more than two years prior and had already begun to read and write. So she began a project to send letters and drawings to the SEAL Team 3 liaison office, through Christy Lansdown.

The activity took her mind off what was going on in Africa. Every time the news came on with special alerts, she jumped, hoping it wasn't something to do with his mission. She didn't know where in Africa he was, so anything that had news of the continent raised her worries.

She had been showing pictures of some of the men on Patrick's squad, but was careful not to pass them around. And last, she showed a picture of Patrick in the box, in full extension, his green keeper jersey hiked up to his waistband. He appeared to be nearly five feet in the air. His large gloved hands were out front, with a few inches separation.

He'd told her stories about that day, and how that game had saved their chance for the playoffs, which they later lost. But for one whole week, the team had basked in the glow of perhaps doing what it hadn't ever done—win their league.

And Patrick had saved the day. Just like he saved her heart, being there where he needed to be. Defending a net was part skill and part luck, he'd told her. He guessed where the ball was going to go by the way the fielder kicked the ball, whether he turned his ankle or toe-kicked it. And some of the better players were adept at looking like they'd kick with one foot and then at the last minute would change, after he'd gotten committed to one direction. She'd seen some recordings of him where he literally looked like a cat adjusting his leap mid-stream.

The Beautiful Game.

It was that. Graceful, gritty, with drama and excitement, defenders blocking, forwards trying to maneuver around anyone to get one nice pass in, perfectly placed to a foot or head, to assist in a goal. But the keeper could take it all away with his body that might nearly span the width of the box, with agility and quick reaction to a ball coming at him forty miles an hour, or more.

The kids were making comments and asking questions.

"So do the SEALs have a soccer team?"

She laughed. "I have no idea. I've never asked him. But I don't think so, because I haven't been washing any grass stains recently."

"What does he like to do the best?"

That was an easy one. "He likes to jump out of airplanes. He likes to watch the little cars and houses down below get bigger and bigger as he falls through the air. And you know what he told me?"

The class wanted to know.

"He said it doesn't feel like falling. It feels like you're balancing on a huge blast of air coming up from the earth to hold you suspended. Isn't that neat?"

The wonderful thing about this age group was that it didn't take much to impress them. Boys and girls alike could relate to adventure and saving the day, and many of their fathers and mothers also served in the military, so her audience was an easy one.

She kissed her phone and prayed for a picture or a message from him every night before she went to bed. There was so much she wanted to do when he came back. She found herself making mental lists of those when she couldn't sleep.

Just go on with your everyday life was easier to say

than do. But the other wives never left her alone. From the first night Patrick was gone, someone from the squad had called her each day, and everyone offered to help her cook or shop or have coffee.

Jake Harmon dropped by several times to make a happy call. Sometimes he brought her a plant for the little garden she was starting in the back. Other days, he brought her favorite coffee. Sometimes he'd just appear on the beach behind her when she went to meditate.

One day, he sat beside her.

"Hi, Jake."

"You hear anything from Patrick?"

"Not yet. How about Tyson?"

"Nope."

She could tell something was on his mind. "Are you worried?'

"I know they know what they're doing. He's smart, like Patrick. Like Ryan."

She stiffened when she heard his name. It had been a few weeks since she'd thought about him, and she made a mental note to call the Rosens and check in.

"What was he really like over there?"

"Ryan? He was fearless." Jake followed it up with a sneer as the sun caught his eyes at the wrong angle.

"You're a bad liar, Jake," she said back to him.

"No, it's truth, man. Funny thing is, if we're scared,

we don't tell each other. We make a joke." He shook his head and started to laugh.

"What? I want to know."

"I can't, man. I really can't. I have a sick sense of humor. You have to sometimes."

"Is this about Ryan, some family secret I should not know?"

"Nah. I'm not telling."

She directed her gaze back out to sea. "So beautiful here. When you come home, do you enjoy it, or are you guarding yourself for the next round?"

"I enjoy the good times. I learn who to hang around and who to avoid. It's a closed circle because no one else understands us. On missions, it's different. We work with lots of people from all over. You don't know them or their background. So you just focus on the job. You spend all your time trying to dovetail into whatever it is that's the goal."

"So who do you hang around?"

"Well, I kinda like you, but you're married. Ryan was my buddy. I was recovering from a busted ankle on this last rotation of his. I wish I'd been there. Maybe I could have saved him."

"You miss him?"

"I sure do. WhooYa Special Operator Ryan!" he shouted to the clouds above them.

"You're still not going to tell me that story?"

"What story?"

"The one you couldn't tell me."

He put his arm around her and then pulled it away just as fast. "You gotta promise you won't tell his parents, right?"

"Sure."

"Or Patrick?"

"Not sure I can promise that. He is my husband, after all."

He took in a deep breath. "Well, here goes. We were in this little village, and there was this six or seven-year-old kid who kept hanging around us. He had a pet goat he was trying to save from his parent's dinner table. So everywhere the boy went, the goat followed. Like Mary Had A Little Lamb."

"That's cute."

"One night, the goat appeared in our mess hall. No kid, just the goat. We were worried the kid would come looking for him. Those streets at night were deadly, dangerous. We also worried something had happened to him. So, Markham chose two of us, Ryan and me, to take the goat back to the boy's house. But we weren't to create any attention. We already had the goat, and there wasn't any way to hide that. Markham's idea was to dress one of us up as a woman."

"No."

"Oh yes. It made sense. And Ryan volunteered. We had some women's clothing we kept on hand, and we trussed him up to look like he had big boobs. The ladies over there don't do that, by the way, but it was some dumbass' idea. We wrapped him up with a huge headscarf, but he still looked like Ryan. So we put lipstick on him and used some of it to give him nice pink cheeks."

Stephanie smiled, buried her chin in her knees. That was not a story Ryan would have ever told her.

"Well, there's more. We took this goat toward the kid's house, and we ran across some military-aged males. Ryan and I were packing, for sure. They were looking us over pretty hard, so Ryan reached over and planted a big one right on my kisser. Right here," he said, pointing to his lips. He shook his head. "That crazy dude." He kept shaking his head.

"Did you make it to the boy's house?"

"We did. When the kid's mother took one look at Ryan, she grabbed the goat and slammed the door. I guess they don't go doing that over there very much."

It warmed her heart to hear the story.

"When we got back to camp, I had red lipstick all over my face and ever after that the guys kept teasing us, "When are you two getting married?"

She chuckled into her hand.

"And for the record, I don't care what the hell people do nowadays. But who do you know who can say they've kissed their best friend on the lips?"

CHAPTER 21

THEY HAD A layover in Djibouti until their transport into Central Africa was arranged. A joint task force was monitoring rebel and militia groups who moved fluidly between the borders of Chad, Niger, and other border countries. Accidents and mistaken identities happened every day. The unnecessary bloodshed was a way of life. But the task force didn't want to drop the SEALs right in the middle of the storm.

A new complication arose when the Deputy Chief of Mission, Connie Renquist, was declared missing, along with her driver. It had all the earmarks of a kidnap for ransom and an assessment was being made whether the abductors, if there were any, even knew Connie was State Department.

Several of the men on Kyle's team had worked with two Security Agents at the Mission, who had transitioned from the Navy to State as part of the

Ambassador and Embassy staff protective detail. Kyle was pleased they would meet them upon arrival.

The Mission staff arranged two transport trucks to meet them in a remote location south of the city of Abuja, where they could be dropped in at midnight.

Twenty-four were to be released in two groups of twelve and meet up at the rendezvous to get the vehicles. Kyle and Cooper led one group of twelve, and they took Patrick with them. T.J., Armando, Fredo, Tyson, and several others were to be dropped about five miles away. Both areas, upon last intel, were reported quiet.

But the mission started off bad from the start. The infrared flares that were supposed to be left for the pilots as markers were turned off. Based on the terrain, they jumped into two locations that resembled the topography on their maps.

But they'd miscalculated.

They were ten miles from where the trucks were located, and instead of being sent to a remote area, they were dropped at the private gardens and animal preserve of a beautiful estate. Kyle radioed and was told it belonged to one of the largest warlords in the region, Mohammed Cunanon. The wealthy Egyptian banker was an arms dealer, and not a friend of the U.S..

"Fuck! Well, we got one more barrier to cross and a lot more terrain to cover. Just another great day in the neighborhood," barked Kyle.

With their night vision and Invisios, the two groups pooled together instead of staying smaller and stealthier. The heat footprint would be a risk, but they were literally surrounded by a jungle of wild animals. Most of the large cats were not separated by cages, and roamed the perimeter checking them out. Their eyes glowed in the night like diamonds.

"I think they know I'm more a dog person, what do you think?" teased Fredo.

"No, I think it's your body odor. If you'd shower now and then—" Coop was interrupted by Kyle's arm on his shoulder.

"Fuck you!" whispered Fredo, trying to get the last word in.

"I'm going to have someone's ass when we get back to Djibouti," whispered Kyle. "We got to get to those trucks before sunrise, and I don't see how the hell we can make that."

In normal and familiar terrain, ten miles would be no problem, even with all their gear and at night. But having to skirt buildings and farms they didn't recognize and do it quietly without detection in a foreign country where the natives shot first and asked questions second was a whole other thing. Making it worse, there were no known friendlies in the area.

Coop extracted his new drone and changed the setting and lens for night. He clicked the little switch, and Patrick heard the whir of a tiny motor running inside the device. He swung his long arm over his head and behind, ran ten feet, and launched it into the sky. He quickly adjusted his tracker screen and got the drone in his control, sending it back and around them in one large swing.

The images that came back indicated there was a sizeable force with vehicles and stores, probably private security, right behind them, still inside the perimeter walls.

"What do you think?" Kyle asked him.

"I don't like our choices," answered Coop. "I can get one of those trucks to start. No guarantee I pick one that works, though. And most of those Russian-made things are noisy as hell. They'd clear out of the dorm or whatever that is, and we'd be caught in the cross."

"Fredo, can we jam them up?" Kyle asked.

"Sure. I mean, they're all in one place."

"Make them run after something. Armando, could you pick a couple drivers off?"

Armando pointed to a storage shed flat roof top. "I'd get good vantage here. But which way do we go? Looks like the gate is here." He pointed to a large sentry station with an active heat signature showing two guards at the entrance. But the entrance was in the opposite direction to where they were headed.

"We could blow the back wall," added Fredo.

"Nah, I want to leave without them knowing we were here, somehow. I just want them to think one of their own borrowed a couple of trucks," said Kyle.

"Maybe we have the Head Shed create a diversion outside?" suggested Coop.

T.J. asked Coop to reposition the drone near the road north that led to the capitol. With little markers in a row bordered by a large square building, he directed Coop to zoom in.

"Just what I thought. That's a Catholic church. That's a graveyard."

Patrick could see that it was flat, there were no big barriers or fences, and it probably wasn't guarded very heavily. The church itself had a small light inside, candles, he thought.

Out of the corner of his eye, Patrick caught a view of a perfectly manicured soccer field built on the grounds. A cart filled with balls was stored beside one of the cages, covered in a tarp.

"Let me ask you something," he started. "Fredo, could you rig something that would ignite on impact and make a fireball?"

"Sure. I got plenty of goodies. How would we get out of the way in time?"

"Can you rig something I can kick that won't take my foot and ankle with it? Something that had some kind of delay? Cause I can kick a well-inflated ball almost eighty yards."

Fredo examined his feet. "It would be easier if we had an air drop, but if I rig something for impact, then yes, it might explode when you kicked it."

"I kick it from underneath, like scooping it up, I can get it maybe fifty plus yards. Maybe more."

"It's worth a try," said Kyle. "They take off in their trucks, and we wait outside the gate and pick off a couple."

"And we head north to the road across the church property. Look, it borders the main road," said T.J.

"What do I use to re-seal the soccer balls afterwards?" Fredo asked.

"Duct Tape," several of them said at once.

Even Patrick had a couple of rolls.

They all rechecked their batteries and Invisios, coordinated their times, checked their weapons, and repositioned knives, rope, and sidearms for quick and easy use in case of close combat. Not everyone brought an M4.

Fredo and Coop made the mixture, setting it carefully in little sandwich bags and bubble wrap, double knotting it with rubber bands. Armando had gone off in search of another rooftop closer to the entrance, taking Danny Begay. Within minutes, they messaged ready.

The balls were carefully filled, sealed, and piled up in the cart. Coop relaunched the drone, and they searched for a target and found the perfect one.

Just outside the complex was an airstrip. And on that airstrip was a very expensive private jet.

"Ladies, I think we have our target," whispered Kyle.

"You gonna shoot down that pretty bird?" Danny messaged back over the Invisio.

"I'm thinking it will get their attention. What do you think? Looks like it belongs to Mr. Cunanan himself," answered Kyle. He left word that they were going to blow up a plane in order to get transport to the meeting point and got final approval.

Patrick took a couple of practice kicks with balls they didn't fill, since he hadn't used those skills for nearly a year. When he picked up the first missile, he didn't like the feel of it.

"Whoa. We got to put more air in this one. Maybe all of them." He rummaged for a pump inside the ball bag and found an expensive French device and gently inflated each ball until he liked the tightness of the leather. "Here goes."

The team immediately backed away from him as he held the soccer ball, let it drop, and kicked it on the underside, just like he'd planned, which made it go high and long, but not fast. He was known for those floaters, which would give his forwards time to get down field.

Fredo whistled.

The ball hit the right wing of the jet with a cracking noise as if the fiberglass body was damaged. The ball bounced off, landed underneath, hit the underside of the jet on the second bounce, and then rolled to a stop at the landing gear. Within seconds, it became a huge fireball. A minute later, the entire plane was engulfed.

"Now that was a nice score, Patrick," said Kyle. "Get ready, Armando and Danny."

"Roger that."

"You want another one?" Patrick asked.

"Fredo, are these dangerous to carry?"

"Well, you can see they did—what?—three, four hops. Not sure all of them are like that, but I think we could take a couple."

Kyle leaned over to him, "When we get a truck, you load the whole basket in the back. I like the way you think, goalkeeper!" He gave Patrick a nice pat on the back.

The sound of electronic communicators squawked and echoed throughout the huge grounds. Several men in pajamas and tee shirts ran for trucks with rifles over their shoulders. Several got through the gate, but the last two Jeep-like vehicles were a good distance behind. With sounds of revving motors and men yelling to organize a fire brigade, the two little cracks from Danny and Armando's sniper rifles were barely heard. Both vehicles slowly headed for the wall and stopped with their drivers dead or wounded.

The team disposed of three additional passengers, quickly loaded up the soccer balls, jumped inside, and headed for the gate and down toward the church. At the last minute, Danny and Armando jumped aboard.

Patrick watched the balls carefully.

By the time they got to their rendezvous point, they were only an hour behind.

"Well, so much for being stealth," T.J. said between chortles. "Why, we were in and out, and no one knew we were there. We didn't leave a footprint. We left a crater."

CHAPTER 22

THE TEST WAS positive. There was no denying it. She stared at it as if it would change the outcome.

How could this happen?

Well, they weren't using anything for protection, but their lovemaking had been very sporadic, and it seemed like a month had gone by without any sex at all. Patrick had been tired from all the PT. The stress had dampened their libido and interfered with their sleeping.

But she blushed when she thought about some of the make-up events they'd had. The intensity had perhaps made-up for the lack of numbers. They even joked that the sparse times were created so they could come crashing back together again. There wasn't a square inch of her body that hadn't been loved, kissed, sucked, or fondled. He commanded everything she had and caused her to want to give him even more.

But this? This might be seen as a betrayal. Or he

might think she'd wanted to talk about starting a family as a ruse since she was already trying to get pregnant. And what would she say to him when he called?

When the phone rang, she was hoping it wasn't him. She hadn't prepared herself for what she had to say. Thankfully, it was Lizzie.

"You ready for a girls' night?" the beautiful blonde asked.

"I'm tired, Lizzie. I can't do a late night."

"Oh heck no. Some soup and French bread? Salad?"

"That sounds great. Where will I meet you?"

"Let's go to the Scupper. We might see some of Coop and Patrick's friends."

"What about the kids?"

"I dropped them over at Christy's. Brandon is having a birthday party, and she said they could spend the night."

She agreed to the meet and took a shower, changed her clothes, and checked her phone for messages. It had been a week, and there had been no word from Patrick. No one had heard anything from the Team.

On her way out, the bedroom she caught the scent of Patrick coming from the closet. Sliding open the door, she found an old keeper jersey and several of his jackets and shirts he'd worn once, still with aftershave and the scent of soap on them. His favorite leather bomber jacket hung like a sad abandoned toy. Her fingers clutched the worn black leather, bringing it up to her nose where she inhaled after closing her eyes. She felt his presence as if he was standing there at her side. Hot tears slowly dribbled down her cheeks while she swayed to some silent music, holding the jacket to her chest and wrapping the long sleeves around her back and waist.

Unable to put it away, she slipped it over her tee shirt, put her hair up in a clip, and rolled back the cuffs a whole six inches so her arms wouldn't drown in it. He was going to go with her wherever she went tonight. She didn't want to be alone.

Lizzie wasn't there when she arrived at the Scupper, but she found Jake and Trevor Markham and several other SEALs from Team 5 and approached their table.

"There she is. We were just talking about you," said Markham. Jake saluted her with his long neck. Markham yelled for another beer for her, and she corrected the order with mineral water.

"I'm exhausted. New school year. The kids seem to get more energy the more I teach. What's up with that?" She leaned into the table and noticed everyone there had dropped their jaw.

"What is it?"

Markham cleared his throat. "Ma'am, with all due

respect, these guys are a little overcome with your beauty."

She blushed and started to say something when she saw their eyes focus on Lizzie coming up behind her. "Hey, fellas." Lizzie put her arm around Stephanie's shoulder, grabbed an unfinished beer from the middle of the table, and took a sip.

"I'll get you one," said Jake, brightly.

"I'm good. Steph and I are going to just have some comfort food in a quiet corner. We're not here to cause trouble." She winked at Spencer, who still hadn't closed his mouth.

"Thanks for the save," Stephanie whispered as they walked to the small dining room at the rear.

A hostess followed them down the narrow hallway memorialized by patches from Teams and police and fire departments from all over the world. There were some campaign flags, even a patch from World War II. Over the bar used to be pictures of fallen SEALs until their numbers got too big to display, so the cards and signed pictures of men lost or grave stones covered the four walls of the small dining area. It was a living monument, Stephanie noted, to the men and women who had pledged to keep her safe, even if they couldn't save themselves. It was part of the culture, and it would be forever changing as the years went by.

She took a huge gulp of water and wrapped herself

in Patrick's jacket, suddenly shivering. Lizzie seemed not to notice. "You want some French fries?"

Stephanie felt like she was going to heave. Pieces of the puzzle were fitting in now. How she'd not just been bored with Patrick being gone, but she was tired too. And that she'd just discovered today, was because of the pregnancy. Maybe it was time to share the news, even at the risk of it getting back to him before she could tell him.

"I'm not very hungry for anything greasy. A nice bowl of soup like you mentioned and their killer French bread would be awesome."

"Share a salad?"

She shrugged and nodded her head.

After their food arrived, Lizzie studied her. "Everything okay?" She frowned and pointed to the jacket with her fork. "Isn't that—?"

"Yes." She pushed away her soup, which she'd barely touched. Wrapping her arms around herself, she shivered again and searched the room for an open window but found none. "What did you do when you found out that you were pregnant with Jameson's child?"

Lizzy's eyes got huge. "Are you? Could this be?"

Stephanie nodded.

Lizzie rushed around the table and gave her a big hug. "Oh, I'm so happy for you."

"He doesn't know yet. No one knows. I want to keep it that way until they come home."

"Oh, you gotta tell him when he calls," she said as she sat back down.

"No, and don't you tell Jameson, either. We were supposed to talk first."

"He'll be thrilled. I know he will."

She grabbed Lizzie's wrist on the wooden tabletop. "Please. Let me do this my way. Will you promise me? It's really important."

"You're not thinking about—"

"No. I'd never do that. It's just that we agreed to talk. I want to stick to the rules with Patrick. I want to play fair. He expects me to be that way. He likes people who keep their word, and I'm no exception."

"Oh heck, Steph, babies come when they're ready. I mean, what were you thinking would happen? You were having sex. What do you think happens when you have sex?"

She winced at the comment about them having sex. "Well, not so much."

"I don't understand."

"Well, we've been—busy. We rushed the wedding, which I'm okay with. But it seems like we never get into a routine."

Lizzie dug into her salad, shaking her head from side to side. "At least you're married. I didn't have that. I didn't want to tie him down, with all his traveling, until I was ready to tell him."

Stephanie watched her eat. "But how did you deal with it?"

"Your situation is completely different than mine. Jameson hadn't made up his mind to settle down. Patrick has. He married you."

"But now I'm throwing another change his way. We're just now used to all this rapid change around us. We haven't gotten into a routine."

"You mean like a lesson plan or something? You need to do a big checkup on yourself, Steph. Remember what I told you? Don't think so much. It's going to drive you crazy. Some days, there aren't any rainbows. Some days there are. Be thankful for little blessings, like this one. It's all good. Everything depends on your attitude. Otherwise, you're not all-in. Be careful with that line of thinking."

"He said the same thing one time."

"You're someone who can adjust, bend without breaking, Steph. I see someone who can tend for this big guy with legs like tree trunks who can jump like a kangaroo."

Stephanie laughed.

"I'm serious! Nothing is ever perfect. Don't hang on so tight. Don't be so rigid. Go with what you're given. That's what I did, and it paid off. This community will never have a routine to it. They plan and plan and plan. But something always changes, goes wrong. They have to deal with all the chaos and make sense of it, keep each other safe. But you know this isn't nine-to-five." She took Stephanie's hand and squeezed it. "Honey, you'd never like a life like that. You know you wouldn't."

"Thanks, coach."

The two women smiled at each other. Stephanie could tell they'd be friends for decades.

"I'm not your coach, either. If you listened to me, we'd all lose every game. I just know that quitting is not an option. We go forward. Like I said, we celebrate what we can, and we don't dwell on what we can't."

Lizzie had been right, of course. It put everything into perspective, and she was grateful for the advice. Someday, she'd be that rock for some new SEAL wife who would come behind. She'd be able to counsel her wisely.

Back at home, she slipped off her clothes and stood naked, facing the mirror, her hand on her belly. She checked herself from the side view and tried to imagine what she'd look like pregnant, and what it would feel like to have life growing inside her—a tiny life that was parts taken from both of them.

She lit one of the red candles, turned off all the lights, put the jacket back on, and slipped into bed. Patrick's jacket held her securely until she fell asleep.

CHAPTER 23

PATRICK WAS INTRODUCED to the two special agents assigned to the State Department as part of the Embassy security detail. Kyle and several others on the Team had served with them on previous missions in the Middle East. Coop had filled Patrick in on who they were and what they meant to the Team.

"We were delighted when we heard you'd be riding point on this," said Mauray Bowen, former sharpshooter who deployed five times with Kyle's SEAL Team 3.

Kyle also shook Joenelle Washington's hand, who had come to his team after giving up a lucrative NFL career. Some of Washington's sprint records were still undefeated fifteen years later. Coop also explained he'd passed up a shot to try out for the Olympics the year he came aboard. He was stationed in Africa because he married a woman from Kenya he met in college.

"So, what's the news?" Coop asked.

"The ambassador's real sorry about all this. The President asked that he be recalled to Washington for meetings, but he was instructed to get his family out." Washington said. "We aren't looking forward to another Benghazi event."

"I hear you. So anyone know where she's at?" Kyle asked.

Mauray spread a map out on a folding table set up as a temporary meeting room before they started their trek to the capital. "We believe they have a rebel training camp here at Deto. Now, we haven't had any of our guys up north there for nearly twenty years. But the African Union forces have, and they've suffered a lot of casualties. They're ineffective."

"And corrupt," Washington interrupted.

"That too. But that's all we got here. It's a whole continent of formerly stable African states that are now crumbling. No one's in control. But the level of violence is on a huge uptick this year, mostly because of what's going on in this northern region, where we think the rebel camp is."

Coop shook his head. "How far away are these guys from the Mission?"

"Sixty, sixty-five miles. It's a two-hour Jeep ride at best," Maurey said. "Why?"

"Who do you call on when you get into trouble?" asked Kyle.

"We got the AU forces. Some of them are okay. There are some lines they will not cross, some warlords they won't defend us against. They show up, and then ten minutes later, they just disappear into the countryside, and you're left exposed."

Washington offered, "We can get an emergency evac force in about five or six hours from Djibouti."

"It's Benghazi all over again." Patrick could see Kyle was troubled they'd not gotten more information prior to the trip over.

Washington grinned. "And that's why the Ambassador is not in the house."

"I know you're gonna ask, and we don't have the answers yet, but I'll give you a guess. We think this Fortune fellow is behind it. We don't think he knows anything other than she's an American tourist."

"Her driver military?" asked T.J.

Washington shook his head. "No, unfortunately, civilian, local guide. So, yeah, it's only a matter of time before he sells her out trying to save himself or his family."

"So, we assume he knows he's holding a valuable U.S. asset." Kyle was studying the map. "What's around this camp?"

"Mountainous region, with several factions of farmers, or former farmers. Now they all fight to protect their food and their women and kids. But it's a race against time. They won't make it. Fortune has killed or chased out all the Christians in the region. Most of the churches and schools are burned. He relishes burning books too. Anything written in English." Mauray had his arms crossed, surveying the topography with Kyle. "Eventually, he'll take over unless the religious clerics stand up to him."

"And you got Ebola?" asked Coop.

"Not like they do inland farther. But yes, it's here."

"How'd this dude get so strong?" Patrick asked.

"I think that's what we're here to learn, son," Washington answered. "Rather, what you're here to learn. He's getting his money from somewhere. It's not oil. He robs the mines, but not enough to make a big difference. Someone well-funded is helping out. He's getting some cash somewhere. He owns most the Capitol police as well as their Security Police, who are the worst of the worst."

"What about that guy whose plane we blew up?" asked Armando.

"Cunanon? You blew up Cunanon's jet?" Washington was surprised.

"Fireballs from hell," Jameson whispered and slapped Patrick on the back.

"He's going to be dangerous, like a wounded bear." Mauray put his finger on the little town of Deto again. "This is the key, right here. I'm betting she's here, if she's still alive."

"Where is the village of Tengo?" Patrick asked.

Washington abruptly looked up. "How do you know about that place?"

"I played soccer in the U.K. with a kid from there."

"There aren't any kids from there. Everyone was slaughtered. They left the burned-out church and installed the cross upside down, leaving it for everyone to see. All the locals stay away. Scariest place on earth. No one to come back to bury the dead, so some are still hanging there after all this time. That was like ten years ago now."

Maurey asked him how the boy escaped.

"He was with his friend, and I think it was a Muslim family who took him in, and then got him to England."

"That's one lucky kid," someone whispered.

"How far is it between this destroyed village and Deto?" asked Kyle.

"Two miles, maybe three. Easy walk. There's a lake nearby with heavy brush that would give great cover."

"Anyone superstitious?" Kyle asked.

"Ah, fuck. You're not gonna—" Washington's face was wrinkled in horror.

"Can you get us there? We won't make you stay." Kyle grinned back at him.

Maurey leaned forward and surveyed the red wavy

lines and circles they'd marked showing current conflicts. It looked like someone had spilled blood all over the northern part of the map. "The problem isn't getting there. It's getting back alive."

The SEALs left the stolen vehicles under heavy cover, and used the two brand new Suburbans with embassy plates Washington and Bowen had provided. They gingerly transferred the soccer balls and the equipment and then followed behind as the security team led the way.

The landscape along the main highway was littered with car and truck hulls, dead cattle, and roadside stands roasted to cinders. But lush green shrubbery was fast retaking the area. All the trees had been cut and used a century ago, judging from the old stumps Patrick saw. He tried to find something about the country he liked, and concluded that the blue sky, unpolluted, was probably the biggest feature.

The capitol city was laid out with a master plan, which was a shock. But even brand new buildings were abandoned before completion, and occasionally, there would be whole city blocks burned. The government buildings sat across the street from what appeared to be the Chinese embassy with its winged roof line and bright blue tiles. The Mission annex was farther down the street in a building that looked more like a prison.

They were shown to a former barracks building

where they could rest up until the midnight move to Tengo. The toilet facility consisted of a hole dug into the ground with a bucket of powdered lye next to it. There was one sink but everyone was encouraged not to drink the water. Washington asked for help, and soon Danny and T.J. brought four cases of water and placed them in the back of the Suburban.

Patrick and Jameson volunteered to stay awake while the rest took advantage of the stiff canvas cots and green horsehair blankets. Washington would be monitoring the radio and update them as needed, or when they left at midnight.

AT ONE O'CLOCK, the landscape changed and was actually beautiful. Rocky outcroppings shone in the blue moonlight. They could hear sounds of animals scurrying around in the brush. Patrick watched Fredo constantly search for snakes, something he was deathly afraid of. Washington reported there had been no activity on any of the drone sites, so the mission was on. They traveled a slow five miles an hour in the two shiny black vehicles, without the headlights on. Several of the men rode with Washington in his van. Two walked in front of the vehicles to scout the terrain.

At last, they came upon a clearing just past a fork in the road. Beyond the turnoff, Patrick could barely make out the remnants of several structures. Three leathery, dark black forms, looking like strips of dirty rags, were still hanging from an old tree branch. The church, with its cross buried upside down in the dirt just outside the entrance, was unusable since the roof was gone. But there was what appeared to be an old supply store that had half of its metal roof intact, which would give some shelter from the sun and a little from the wind. Old refrigerated cases, completely stripped bare and with their glass tops missing, littered the place.

It would be light in three hours, so Kyle ordered him and Jameson to bed down, took Cooper and Washington to a corner to study maps again, and asked the rest of the squad to chill until sunrise.

At first, Patrick couldn't sleep. He stared up at the stars that were twice as bright as those in San Diego and found the second thing he liked about this country. He closed his eyes and heard Stephanie giggling under his arm and felt the way her hand smoothed down over his skin. He could smell the lavender cream she put on her legs every morning. He could smell the hair entangled in her hairbrush sitting idly by the bathroom sink.

He heard the sounds of the ocean as his feet trekked over the warm white sand. Somewhere a seabird was calling. Then everything went dark.

CHAPTER 24

STEPHANIE WENT FOR an early morning walk on the beach, then stopped by her favorite breakfast coffee shop and read one of her books while drinking herbal tea and having a huge bowl of oatmeal loaded with fresh strawberries. She found a local bookstore and purchased several books on pregnancy and childbirth. She bought a set of tapes on pregnancy for new moms. And lastly, she made an appointment with her doctor.

The blood test confirmed the test was positive. An ultrasound was performed, and the technician guessed she was about eight weeks pregnant.

She walked home with the picture—her first photo to put in the baby book. She embraced everything she had to do, including making plans to search online for baby furniture.

The landlord dropped by later in the week to inform her that they would have to move because she was putting the property on the market. Stephanie suggested that they might be interested in buying it and the owner agreed to wait until Patrick's return.

She planted flowers in the backyard and along the walkway in front. She purchased some small tomato and pepper plants and a cucumber, planting them all at the side of the fence where it would be warmest and get full sun all day.

Lizzie called her to check in.

"Has anyone from the Team called in?" she asked.

"I don't think so. It happens all the time." Lizzie paused. "Things better now?"

"Yes. I've confirmed with the doctor and we think I'm about eight weeks. Thanks for the kick in the pants. It got me into gear."

"You'd have gotten there on your own. Okay, I'm off to a gymnastics tournament."

"Hey, Lizzie, I've still not been told him, so please don't mention anything to anyone until you check with me, okay?"

"Scout's honor."

Stephanie searched color charts and cut out things she wanted to buy for the nursery. She toured the local hospital her doctor used and loved the feel and attitude of staff.

Her parents were thrilled with the news and they swore complete silence. She also called the Rosens and informed them of the news.

She thought of a million ways she could break the news to Patrick when he came home but couldn't decide. A lot would depend on what his state of mind was when he got here.

She even went car shopping, researching something that would be easier with the baby seat than her small car. She registered for a swim class for pregnant moms and even attended her first class.

But every morning it was the same. She looked in the mirror, to try to see if anything at all was showing. Some days she saw the swelling in her belly and on others, it was harder to tell. One thing she did notice was that her breasts were getting sensitive and enlarged. Patrick wouldn't mind that at all.

News reports bothered her less and less. She learned to tune them out instead of running to chase a story flashing across the screen in red. She also found excuses to get together with Kyle's wife and Shannon, T.J.'s wife. Her world had changed. She hoped Patrick would embrace it the same as she had.

Stephanie bought new sheets for the bed and replaced some tattered curtains with new bright white ones. She placed a call to a company to measure her windows for blackout shades she could have installed behind.

Whatever was going to lie ahead, she was ready.

CHAPTER 25

PATRICK AND THE Team explored the Village of the Damned, as it was being called. In the early morning light, it didn't look as ominous as it did the night before. But he didn't blame any of the locals for staying away. It was a grim reminder of man's inhumanity to man. It also was a calling card, preparing them for what they might find in the village at Deto.

He helped Coop and T.J. cut down the three bodies and found a broken hoe to dig a shallow grave for all three of them together. A search of the rest of the village remnants didn't yield anything they could use or any intelligence of value. There were some volunteer corn plants stubbornly attempting to grow in shallow furrows marred by tire tracks and ashes from bonfires.

They opted to leave the vehicles behind and travel through the brush on foot to keep the element of surprise on their side. Fredo sent a radio message about where they were heading and got confirmation they'd be tracked.

Coop sent the drone out, replacing the night vision camera with the one he used for daytime surveillance. He carefully maneuvered it away from any clusters of homes, or buildings, especially if there were vehicles parked outside. After not seeing any trucks packed with troops in the area, they headed towards Deto with the drone as their scout.

Little red bugs got inside Patrick's ankles, traveling up his calf. He cursed that he'd not thought to tie his boots over his pants. The little critters stung and then itched. One or two others had the same thing going on, but the group stayed together, hanging under the cover of trees, which were getting larger and larger the closer they got north.

"Kyle," Coop whispered.

Everyone gathered around his screen. Due north was an encampment along the edge of a fairly good-sized lake. A large two-story building with bars on the windows was in the center of a clearing. As the drone adjusted focus, they could see a sign hanging at an angle, ready to fall to the ground.

Deto University.

"What the hell?" Coop asked Washington.

"The government claims to have built seventeen colleges with money they got from the U.N.. We could never find one for the nearly billion dollars they got."

"So, is this the source of their funds? This is no billion-dollar building." Kyle was stating the obvious.

"Looks like one of the Spanish prisons in Puerto Rico," Armando added. "Built for the slave traders originally."

"See if you can get any detail into the windows," asked Kyle.

Coop skillfully adjusted the directional stick, remotely adjusting the camera lens so photographs could be sent to the crew at the embassy in Abuja. From there it could be uploaded to Washington as well as to the joint task force in Djibouti.

"I don't want to get too close," Coop began. "It looks like most of the windows are dark, but… there!"

In the window opening at the upper left of the building, an arm was resting on the sill. The exposed skin was that of a Caucasian male. His torso was in full shade. None of the other windows yielded anything.

Patrick pointed out a pair of black boots sticking out from under an overhang of some kind. They saw an arm waving, and then three people walked out into the bright sunlight, two in African uniforms. One gentleman was walking with a cell phone to his ear. When he finished his call, he lowered the phone, revealing the image of a lion tattooed on his cheek.

"Fuckin' Johnathan Fortune."

Coop sent the upload for identification and the call came back that it was indeed the warlord. He was asked to try to get a picture of anyone else nearby. Coop adjusted the angle again, swung around so that the sun was behind the drone, and got a shot of the faces of Fortune's guests. The other man wore a uniform similar to Fortunes, but the third one, a much smaller man, was in civilian clothes with dark hair and appeared oriental.

A green Russian-made Jeep pulled up the dusty road, parking in front of the concrete building and four men got out. Patrick saw several arms and faces appear in the barred windows.

"Coop, I think you've got more prisoners. That's what this appears to be, a prison."

Every one of the faces was Caucasian. Coop scanned them slowly, hoping to get better detail but no one in the group of unfortunates appeared familiar. And none of them resembled Connie.

Washington told them there'd been some chatter about Connie late last night, but the detail was nonspecific.

"Suppose she's injured?" Patrick asked. "She could be housed somewhere else."

They tried to maneuver the drone to get a view of what kind of a structure was under the overhang, but the shadows were too long. The Asian man looked up to the sky.

"Oops. I might have been seen," Coop muttered. "I'm bringing her home."

Fortune aimed a pistol at the camera. The men heard the crack of the firearm, but the drone had banked, returning to their position. It landed with little problem just like a model airplane. Coop quickly slid the body of the drone out from the slit in the single wing piece, placed the two parts in his gun cloth, and rolled then tied them up together. He placed them in his backpack, alongside the monitor.

"So much for the element of surprise," Kyle muttered.

"He's going to figure someone is out here and will check it out. I say we split up," offered Washington.

Kyle agreed, waving Armando and Danny forward to scout out a spot they could give cover. They disappeared into the brush without a sound.

"We should wait until dark," said Washington.

"I agree, but we don't have that much time. I just hope they aren't working with the Egyptian. They'd be expecting a night raid, so we have to go in now. Besides, this isn't heavily fortified. We outnumber them. This might be the first truck in a convoy and then we'd be fucked."

The sound of a high-powered rifle got the Team's attention. Coop and Fredo looked at each other and shook their heads. "Kyle, that's not Danny or Armando," Fredo reported.

Their LPO split them quickly into four-man teams, sending them to different corners of the complex. He asked them to identify positions to the shooters to avoid a mishap but also to be a source of information about targets. He sent Jameson and Patrick back to the base camp to stay with the vehicles in case they had visitors, ordering them to stay out of sight. Two other men came with them.

Patrick's group did a fast jog along a dried-up creek bed and then across a field of what used to be well-tilled farmland. They encountered a dead goat with its belly bloated and feet sticking in the air. The animal had been recently shot.

Patrick found evidence of a campsite, the fire still warm, and some bloody rags. But they continued their jog until at last they came upon the edge of Adolphis' old village and hunkered down low in the wild foliage. They could hear the sounds of a vehicle approaching.

Kyle let them know the team was going in to take over the complex. The sounds of automatic fire were at their backs just as the green transport arrived. Scanning the area, Fortune climbed out and four other men trained their rifles on the brush, taking random shots.

"We gotta get out of here," said Jameson.

They rolled to take cover behind a burned-out tree stump and watched the men approach their vehicles.

Fortune peered through the glass on the first one, then walked to the rear of the second, which held the soccer balls.

"Can you get that shot?" he asked Jameson.

"I can," the young shooter agreed, already having them in his sites.

Patrick messaged Kyle. "Can we sacrifice the Suburbans?"

Everyone heard the approval, and within a second, the young kid took dead aim at the gas tanks firing at one and then the other. Fortune ducked, thinking he was the target, just as both vans went up in a fireball ten feet high, and then fell to the ground on top of the shredded bodies of Fortune's crew.

Jameson notified Kyle, and the chatter was all celebration.

"We've cleaned house, too, and have some aid workers. Plus we found Connie. She's injured, but she'll be okay.

After waiting for any other enemy to show up, Patrick and the other three SEALs ran to the scene of the soccer bombs. He took out his camera and held it high in one hand while pouring through the carnage until he found the detached head of the man who killed Adolphis' family. He snapped a picture and sent it off to his friend in London.

It might cost him a future promotion, maybe get him into bigger trouble, but Patrick had to let Adolphis know that the spear had done his job.

CHAPTER 26

THE HOMECOMING WAS spectacular. Stephanie raced to the airfield and parked along the fence with the other dozen or so SEAL wives. She inched over closer to Christy, who was telling them some general details.

"I'm allowed to tell you they got their target and a whole lot of other information, too. Computers, cash, a whole treasure trove of stuff. And they rescued a dozen international aid workers, including two embassy employees. Ladies, they did really good. We should be proud of them."

Several wives hugged each other as Christy sauntered over to speak to Stephanie.

"I have a message for you, sweetie," Christy began. "Your guy was a star. I have no idea what he did, but Kyle said he saved the day."

"Thanks. That was what he always did on his soccer team. I know he'll not tell me, but you let me know if you ever find out." She grabbed Christy and gave her a healthy hug.

"They aren't always this way. Most the time they just walk in the door and we know they're home. This one was special for some reason."

The sound of a bloated body transport was so loud they all covered their ears. The huge plane hovered forever over the runway and then touched down. Stephanie held on to the chain-link fence they were required to stand behind, just like the other ladies present.

One by one, the men ran down the rear ramp and onto the tarmac, and one by one, they ran to the gate guarded by two handsome Marines doing airfield security. The lock was removed, and Stephanie felt arms about her before she saw him.

"Welcome home, hero."

Patrick pressed her so hard into him, she had to push back. "So how's your month been?" he asked as he wrapped his arm around her waist, hoisted his duty bag on his other shoulder, and walked in tandem until they arrived at his truck.

"Oh, pretty normal. But I hope you won't be upset with me."

He started the truck and cocked his head, frowning. "Not possible. What did you do?"

"I was naughty."

"Is that all? Well, Stephanie, I was counting on that. Tell me something I'm not expecting. What other little tricks do you have in your treasure trove?"

She smiled. "You'll see."

Patrick flew them to London for Christmas, like he'd promised. It was festive being in the land of Dickens, and they even caught a live performance of A Christmas Carol. They went antique shopping and found some boutique children's shops, purchasing enough for the new baby to need another suitcase for the trip home.

On Sunday, they had tickets to see the Hotspurs play. The fans were rowdy. The riot police were out in full force, separating the sections from each other, and rotated every twenty minutes. A bus was turned over when an opposing group discovered who was on board.

Adolphis met them outside the locker room. He gave Patrick a hug, tears streaming down his face. Patrick introduced her, and the young man nearly bowed.

"He's da best. Da best goalkeeper ever."

Stephanie was so proud. "I completely agree."

Adolphis screamed and picked Patrick up again in a bear hug. "You did it, man. You got that sonofabitch."

"Not me, the Team. But yes."

She listened to the two athletes share their memories, their history. It wasn't until that moment she realized what the mission had meant to the young man who had barely escaped with his life. Patrick reached into his pocket and pulled out a small foil packet, handing it to Adolphis.

"Here you go, kid. Mission accomplished. I took it with me all through BUD/S. I wore it every day during the training, during the Trident ceremony, and I brought it to Africa with me. It now belongs with you."

The young keeper was overwhelmed, but pushed back the shiny foil package, returning it to Patrick's possession.

"No, man. It's yours. We share this. I have my pages and you have yours. You rid the world of one very bad guy who was responsible for many many families being completely wiped out. This gift, I want you to keep. The blood of my family will protect you forever. Thank you, Paddy, my friend."

"It won't always be like this. There aren't always winners like this time. We were lucky, Steph."

She was tucked under his arm as they stood in the massive oak-paneled suite overlooking Big Ben. "I suspected as much. But what a way to start your new career."

"I wish everyone always came back safe, whole, and the mission achieved. But the world is not like that." He kissed the top of her head.

"Until then, we move on, and we celebrate what we can. Ryan would have liked this," she said.

His slight reflexive inhale told her he hadn't expected that comment. "I have to tell you something, Steph. He was with me. He came with us all. Does that sound nuts?"

"Not at all. If it wasn't for Ryan, you and I would have never met, Patrick."

He shook his head. "Nah. I'd have spotted you and that little pink lunchbox eventually. You were always destined to be mine."

Coming February 2019
SEAL Love's Legacy

ABOUT THE AUTHOR

NYT and USA Today best-selling author Sharon Hamilton's award-winning Navy SEAL Brotherhood series have been a fan favorite from the day the first one was released. They've earned her the coveted Amazon author ranking of #1 in Romantic Suspense, Military Romance and Contemporary Romance categories, as well as in Gothic Romance for her Vampires of Tuscany and Guardian Angels. Her characters follow a sometimes rocky road to redemption through passion and true love.

Now that he's out of the Navy, Sharon can share with her readers that her son spent a decade as a Navy SEAL, and he's the inspiration for her books.

Her Golden Vampires of Tuscany are not like any vamps you've read about before, since they don't go to ground and can walk around in the full light of the sun.

Her Guardian Angels struggle with the human charges they are sent to save, often escaping their vanilla world of Heaven for the brief human one. You won't find any of these beings in any Sunday school class.

She lives in Sonoma County, California with her husband and her Doberman, Tucker. A lifelong organic gardener, when she's not writing, she's getting *verra verra* dirty in the mud, or wandering Farmers Markets looking for new Heirloom varieties of vegetables and flowers. She and her husband plan to cure their wanderlust (or make it worse) by traveling in their Diesel Class A Pusher, Romance Rider. Starting with this book, all her writing will be done on the road.

She loves hearing from her fans:
Sharonhamilton2001@gmail.com

Her website is:
sharonhamiltonauthor.com

Find out more about Sharon, her upcoming releases, appearances and news from her newsletter, **AND receive a free book** when you sign up for Sharon's newsletter.
sharonhamiltonauthor.com/contact/#mailing%20list

Facebook:
facebook.com/SharonHamiltonAuthor

Twitter:
twitter.com/sharonlhamilton

Pinterest:
pinterest.com/AuthorSharonH

Google Plus:
plus.google.com/u/1/+SharonHamiltonAuthor/posts

BookBub:
bookbub.com/authors/sharon-hamilton

Youtube:
youtube.com/channel/UCDInkxXFpXp_4Vnq08ZxMBQ

Soundcloud:
soundcloud.com/sharon-hamilton-1

Sharon Hamilton's Rockin' Romance Readers:
facebook.com/groups/sealteamromance

Sharon Hamilton's Goodreads Group:
goodreads.com/group/show/199125-sharon-hamilton-readers-group

Visit Sharon's Online Store:
sharon-hamilton-author.myshopify.com

Join Sharon's Review Teams:

eBook Reviews:
reviewcrewsh@gmail.com

Audio Reviews:
reviewcrewaudio@gmail.com

Life is one fool thing after another.
Love is two fool things after each other.

SERIES OVERVIEW

SEAL BROTHERHOOD SERIES OVERVIEW
Accidental SEAL (Book #1)
Fallen SEAL Legacy (Book #2)
SEAL Under Covers (Book #3)
SEAL The Deal (Book #4)
Cruisin' For A SEAL (Book #5)
SEAL My Destiny (Book #6)
SEAL Of My Heart (Book #7)
Fredo's Dream (Book 8)
SEAL My Love (Book #9)
SEAL Brotherhood Box Set 1 (Accidental SEAL & Prequel)
SEAL Brotherhood Box Set 2 (Fallen SEAL & Prequel)
Ultimate SEAL Collection Vol. 1 (Books 1-4 + 2 Prequels)
Ultimate SEAL Collection Vol. 2 (Books 5-7)

SILVER SEALS OVERVIEW
SEAL Love's Legacy

SLEEPER SEALS SERIES OVERVIEW
Bachelor SEAL

NEW STAND ALONES

SEAL's Goal: The Beautiful Game
Love Me Tender, Love You Hard

BONE FROG BROTHERHOOD SERIES OVERVIEW

New Year's SEAL Dream (Book #1)
SEALed At The Altar (Book #2)

BAD BOYS OF SEAL TEAM 3 SERIES OVERVIEW

SEAL's Promise (Book #1)
SEAL My Home (Book #2)
SEAL's Code (Book #3)
Big Bad Boys Bundle (Books 1-3)

BAND OF BACHELORS SERIES OVERVIEW

Lucas (Book #1) *Available Only in Audio or Bundle*
Alex (Book #2)
Jake (Book #3)
Jake 2 (Book #4)
Big Band of Bachelors Bundle

NASHVILLE SEALS SERIES OVERVIEW

Nashville SEAL (Book #1)
Nashville SEAL: Jameson (Books 1 2)

TRUE BLUE SEALS SERIES OVERVIEW
True Navy Blue (prequel to Zak)
Zak (Includes novella above)

PARADISE SERIES OVERVIEW
Paradise: In Search of Love

NOVELLAS OVERVIEW
SEAL You In My Dreams (Magnolias and Moonshine)
SEAL Of Time (Trident Legacy)

FALL FROM GRACE SERIES OVERVIEW (PARANORMAL)
Gideon: Heavenly Fall

GOLDEN VAMPIRES OF TUSCANY SERIES OVERVIEW (PARANORMAL)

Honeymoon Bite (Book #1)
Mortal Bite (Book #2)

THE GUARDIANS SERIES OVERVIEW (PARANORMAL)

Heavenly Lover (Book #1)
Underworld Lover (Book #2)
Underworld Queen (Book #3)

AUDIOBOOKS

Sharon Hamilton's books are available as audiobooks narrated by J.D. Hart.

REVIEWS

PRAISE FOR THE
SEAL BROTHERHOOD SERIES

"Fans of Navy SEAL romance, I found a new author to feed your addiction. Finely written and loaded delicious with moments, Sharon Hamilton's storytelling satisfies like a thick bar of chocolate." —Marliss Melton, bestselling author of the *Team Twelve* Navy SEALs series

"Sharon Hamilton does an EXCELLENT job of fitting all the characters into a brotherhood of SEALS that may not be real but sure makes you feel that you have entered the circle and security of their world. The stories intertwine with each book before…and each book after and THAT is what makes Sharon Hamilton's SEAL Brotherhood Series so very interesting. You won't want to put down ANY of her books and they will keep you reading into the night when you should be sleeping. Start with this book…and you will not want to stop until you've read the whole series and then…you will be waiting for Sharon to write the next one." (5 Star Review)

"Kyle and Christy explode all over the pages in this first book, *[Accidental SEAL],* in a whole new series of SEALs. If the twist and turns don't get your heart jumping, then maybe the suspense will. This is a must read for those that are looking for love and adventure with a little sloppy love thrown in for good measure." (5 Star Review)

PRAISE FOR THE
BAD BOYS OF SEAL TEAM 3 SERIES

"I love reading this series! Once you start these books, you can hardly put them down. The mix of romance and suspense keeps you turning the pages one right after another! Can't wait until the next book!" (5 Star Review)

"I love all of Sharon's Seal books, but *[SEAL's Code]* may just be her best to date. Danny and Luci's journey is filled with a wonderful insight into the Native American life. It is a love story that will fill you with warmth and contentment. You will enjoy Danny's journey to become a SEAL and his reasons for it. Good job Sharon!" (5 Star Review)

PRAISE FOR THE
BAND OF BACHELORS SERIES

"*[Lucas]* was the first book in the Band of Bachelors series and it was a phenomenal start. I loved how we got to see the other SEALs we all love and we got a look at Lucas and Marcy. They had an instant attraction, and their love was very intense. This book had it all, suspense, steamy romance, humor, everything you want in a riveting, outstanding read. I can't wait to read the next book in this series." (5 Star Review)

PRAISE FOR THE
TRUE BLUE SEALS SERIES

"Keep the tissues box nearby as you read *True Blue SEALs: Zak* by Sharon Hamilton. I imagine more than I wish to that the circumstances surrounding Zak and Amy are all too real for returning military personnel and their families. Ms. Hamilton has put us right in the middle of struggles and successes that these two high school sweethearts endure. I have read several of Sharon Hamilton's military romances but will say this is the most emotionally intense of the ones that I have read. This is a well-written, realistic story with authentic characters that will have you rooting for them and proud of those who serve to keep us safe. This is an author who writes amazing stories that you love and cry with the characters. Fans of Jessica Scott and Marliss Melton will want to add Sharon Hamilton to their list of realistic military romance writers." (5 Star Review)

Made in the USA
San Bernardino, CA
31 October 2018